Dear Reader,

When I think of Italy, I naturally think of beautiful cities, amazing countryside, delicious food and romance. When I visited years ago I was constantly enthralled by the history of the country, the gorgeous architecture, beautiful sculptures and paintings, and the warmth of the Italian people. I loved it! I want to go again.

But until that time comes I've settled for spending a few months with Cristiano and Mariella as they meet each other and begin to fall in love.

The setting is the countryside near Naples, with only one trip to Rome, revolving around the beauty of the area, the delicious food and the delights of love as they begin to realize each is perfect for the other—despite feeling they can't break free of their pasts.

Come feel the warmth of Italy and the magic of falling in love with two special people.

All the best

Barbara

## THE BRIDES
*of*
## BELLA ROSA

*Romance, rivalry and a family reunited.*

For years Lisa Firenzi and Luca Casali's
sibling rivalry has disturbed the quiet, sleepy Italian
town of Monta Correnti, and their two feuding
restaurants have divided the market square.

Now, as the keys to the restaurants are
handed down to Lisa's and Luca's children,
will history repeat itself? Can the next generation
undo its parents' mistakes, reunite the families
and ultimately join the two restaurants?

Or are there more secrets to be revealed…?

*The doors to the restaurants are open,
so take your seats and look out for secrets,
scandals and surprises on the menu!*

# BARBARA McMAHON

*Firefighter's Doorstep Baby*

THE BRIDES *of* BELLA ROSA

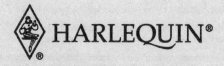

HARLEQUIN®

TORONTO • NEW YORK • LONDON
AMSTERDAM • PARIS • SYDNEY • HAMBURG
STOCKHOLM • ATHENS • TOKYO • MILAN • MADRID
PRAGUE • WARSAW • BUDAPEST • AUCKLAND

Recycling programs
for this product may
not exist in your area.

ISBN-13: 978-0-373-17692-2

FIREFIGHTER'S DOORSTEP BABY

First North American Publication 2010

Copyright © 2010 by Harlequin Books S.A.

*Special thanks and acknowledgment are given to Barbara McMahon for her contribution to the Brides of Bella Rosa series.*

This edition published by arrangement with Harlequin Books S.A.

For questions and comments about the quality of this book please contact us at Customer_eCare@Harlequin.ca.

www.eHarlequin.com

**Printed in U.S.A.**

**Barbara McMahon** was born and raised in the south U.S.A., but settled in California after spending a year flying around the world for an international airline. After settling down to raise a family and work for a computer firm, she began writing when her children started school. Now, feeling fortunate in being able to realize a long-held dream of quitting her "day job" and writing full-time, she and her husband have moved to the Sierra Nevada mountains of California, where she finds her desire to write is stronger than ever. With the beauty of the mountains visible from her windows, and the pace of life slower than the hectic San Francisco Bay Area where they previously resided, she finds more time than ever to think up stories and characters and share them with others through writing. Barbara loves to hear from readers. You can reach her at P.O. Box 977, Pioneer, CA 95666-0977, U.S.A. Readers can also contact Barbara at her website: www.barbaramcmahon.com.

*To First Responders everywhere—thanks for all you do to serve and protect every day. FDNY, we will never forget.*

# CHAPTER ONE

MARIELLA HOLMES stood on the small stone patio and gazed at the lake. Some daredevil was racing the wind on a Jet Ski. A spume of water arced behind it. The soft rumble of its engine faded as it sped across the surface of the water. She glanced into the cottage. Dante was still sleeping. She looked back at the reckless idiot on the Jet Ski; if the noise had woken the baby she'd have been more than annoyed. It had taken her longer than usual to get him to sleep.

What was the maniac doing anyway? If he fell in the water he'd be frozen in no time. Late October was so not lake weather. Yet even as she watched, she felt a spark of envy. He looked carefree skimming along at warp speed. If he was on vacation, he was certainly making the most of his time.

She gazed around the tree-covered hills that rose behind the lake. This would be lovely in the summer. She could picture children swimming in the water, canoes or rowboats dotting the surface. Imagine even more daredevils testing their skills with the Jet Skis; chasing the excitement, exploring the limits of their skills. Her gaze drawn back to the man, she continued to watch as she hoped this one wouldn't crash. There was beauty in the arc of water spewing from behind him, in the soft wake that radiated from the path of the Jet Ski. Sunshine sparkled on the water, causing a misty rainbow when he turned.

She pulled her sweater closer and drank in the clean mountain air. Beautiful and peaceful. She had never visited this area before. She hadn't known what to expect. Forested hills, quiet lakes, small villages. It was enchanting. She wished she could explore everything, but they wouldn't be here that long. Whichever way things went, it would be a relatively short visit. She'd had a lull in work and so had acted on the spur of the moment when she'd decided to come see where Dante's father was from.

A loud smack of the Jet Ski on the water as it bounced over its own wake had her drawn again to the man. At this distance she could only see the dark hair and broad shoulders as he sat astride the machine. He seemed fearless as the engine roared louder and he went even faster. She could imagine herself flying along, the wind blowing all cares away.

Shivering, she stepped back inside the cottage. This would have been a perfect chance to call Ariana, tell her how much she was enjoying Lake Clarissa, and that she'd seen a man who fired her imagination. She still couldn't believe her best friend would never call her up again to talk a mile a minute about life. Would never get to hold her son or watch him learn to walk or start school. Mariella brushed the sudden tears from her cheeks. Ariana had been there for her when her own parents had died, but she was not here now. It was Mariella's turn to step up to the plate.

Time healed all hurts, Mariella knew that. She had gotten over the worst of her grief after her parents' untimely death when she'd been in New York during her first year at university. Her grief over Ariana's death would gradually ease too. She knew in her mind she'd remember her friend with love as the years went on. But sometimes she felt raw, burning pain. Ariana had only been twenty-two. Her life should have stretched out until they were both old ladies. Instead, it had ended far too soon.

Shaking her head to dislodge depressing thoughts, Mariella focused on the future. She had Dante. She had a job. She had a quest. One day at a time. It had worked so far. So what if she felt overwhelmed some days? Caring for an unexpected baby wasn't easy. At least they were both healthy, well fed and comfortable. And she was getting the hang of being a mother. She hoped Dante would never remember her inept first attempts.

Crossing the small living room, she checked on the infant sleeping in the baby carrier still locked in the stroller. Checking the time, she knew he'd awaken soon for a bottle. She had a few minutes to unpack the groceries she'd brought and prepare his next meal before the first stirring.

She'd booked the room for a week, thinking that would be enough time to wander around and get a feel for the place and see if anyone here recognized the picture she had of Ariana. If not, they'd move on to Monta Correnti. She had no firm clues, no certainty she was even in the right place. She only knew this was the place Ariana had spoken about. The only clue she had given about Dante's father.

Ariana had been so sick and afraid those last weeks. Mariella wished her friend had called upon her earlier, but she had waited until graduation and Mariella's return to Rome before sharing the prognosis for the disease that ravaged her body. And, despite all Mariella's pleading, she had not revealed Dante's father's name. Only the bare fact that he came from this area, and they'd spent a wonderful weekend at Lake Clarissa.

The only child of older parents, Mariella was now alone in the world—and the guardian of an infant to boot. She'd always wished for brothers and sisters, aunts, uncles and cousins galore. She wished that for Dante as well. Maybe she could find his father, tell him of his son and discover he came from a large loving family who would take the baby into their hearts.

She glanced over to him again, her heart twisting. She loved this child. But it was so hard to be suddenly a mom. If she found his father, would she be able to give the baby up? Would a big family be best for him? She was still uncertain. At least she didn't have to make any decisions today. First she had to see if she could even locate his father. She'd decide then what course of action to take.

Cristiano opened the throttle full blast as the Jet Ski skimmed across the waves. The air was chilled, causing his blood to pump harder to keep him warm. The thrill of speed, the challenge of control, the sun glittering on the water all made him feel more alive than he had in months. All other thoughts and worries and memories evaporated. If the Jet Ski could go even faster, he would have relished the exhilaration, however short-lived. He pushed the machine to the max.

The injured ankle had healed. He'd been unable to use the Jet Ski during the warm summer weeks, but now, in the waning days of fall, he had the lake to himself. Power roared beneath him as he bounced over the small waves. The shore blurred by as he pushed the throttle surging to that last bit of power. He felt invincible. He'd cheated death once this year. He would not be taken today.

Drawing near the shore, he slowly banked toward the right, not sharp enough to capsize, but enough to swerve away from the rocky land that was fast approaching. He could ease back on the throttle, but what challenge was in that?

The Jet Ski bumped over its own wake and he stood up

to cushion the smacks as it slammed down on the water. Now his ankle ached a bit, reminding him he was not yet totally fit. Another circle and he'd return to the dock. It was cold enough that his toes were going numb. But there were few enough sunny days at this time of year. He'd take all he could get to enjoy being on the lake.

A few moments later, he slowed the ski and made a figure eight, then angled near the shore to make a big sweep that would take him back to the dock. Lake Clarissa was empty, the beach deserted. He was the only person in sight. The summer tourists had long left and the few people who came in the winter had not yet shown up. He had the place to himself.

As he skied past the row of cottages the Bertatalis rented, he noticed the far one was occupied. Lake Clarissa didn't offer the nightlife that Monta Correnti did. Most people weren't foolish enough to venture into the cold lake at this time of year. They had more sense than he did. It was probably some older couple who wanted to watch birds or see the leaves change. It wasn't that far to Monta Correnti they couldn't still drive over for some nighttime entertainment.

He pulled the Jet Ski up to the dock and in only moments secured it in the small floating ramp in the berth he rented. He tied it down and headed back to land. His wet feet left footprints on the wooden dock as he walked to his motorcycle. Drying himself, he quickly donned the jeans and boots he'd left across the seat, and pulled on a heavy sweater. It felt good to get warm. Donning the helmet, he mounted the bike and kick-started it. The rumble was not unlike the Jet Ski. Did power equate noise? He laughed at that idea and pulled onto the street. The small amount of traffic still surprised him after his time in Rome. Vacations in Lake Clarissa had always been fleeting, too much work waiting at home when he'd been a child. Once grown, he'd preferred his exciting life travelling the world with his job, or the challenges of extreme sports, to spending much time in this little sleepy lakeside village.

Until the bombing had altered everything.

Shortly after one Cristiano got off his motorcycle on the side street by Pietro's Bistro. Lunch here would beat cooking for himself. His father would be horrified his own son didn't like cooking. It wasn't that he didn't like it precisely, it just didn't seem worth the effort for only one.

There was a wide patio for dining, empty this time of year. It wasn't that cool, yet the breezes blowing down from the higher elevation carried a chill. He entered the warm restaurant and paused a moment while his eyes got used to the dimmer light. Pietro's smelled like home. The restaurant he'd worked in most of his childhood, that his father still owned, was even of a similar rustic theme. Bella Rosa had more patrons and more bustle than Pietro's, but Pietro's was free of the ties to Cristiano's past he was trying to flee.

There were couples and groups eating at various tables—it was more crowded than he'd expected. Some people he recognized and nodded to when they looked up and waved. When Emeliano appeared from the kitchen, white apron tied neatly around his waist, heavy tray balanced on one hand, Cristiano watched. His arms almost ached at the remembered tiredness he'd felt after a long day at Rosa. He hadn't worked there in years, but some memories didn't fade. Even when he wished they would.

"Cristiano, sit anywhere. I'll be there soon," Emeliano called out as he deftly transferred the tray from his hand to the stand beside the table he was serving.

Cristiano walked toward his favorite table, near the big window overlooking the town square. It was occupied.

He walked past and sat at the next one, then looked at the woman who had taken the table he liked best.

She had blonde hair with copper highlights. She was cooing to a small baby and seemed oblivious to the rest of the restaurant. He didn't recognize her. Probably another tourist. Even keeping to himself, he still kept tapped into the local rumor mill—enough to know if someone local had a new baby visiting. Italian families loved new babies.

The woman looked up and caught his gaze. She smiled then looked away.

He stared at her feeling that smile like a punch to the gut. From that quick glimpse he noted her eyes were silver, her cheeks brushed with pink—from the sun or the warmth of the restaurant? Glancing around, he wondered idly where her husband was.

"Rigatoni?" Emeliano asked when he stopped by Cristiano's table, distracting Cristiano from his speculation about the woman.

"Sure." He ordered it almost every time he ate here.

"Not as good as what you get at Rosa," Emeliano said, jotting it on a pad.

"I'm not at Rosa," Cristiano said easily. He could have quickly covered the distance between Lake Clarissa and Monta Correnti for lunch, but he wasn't ready to see his family yet. Sometimes he wondered if he'd ever be ready to go back home.

"Saw you on the lake. You could get killed."

He and Emeliano had played together as kids, challenging each other to swim races, exploring the hills with his brother Valentino. Cristiano grinned up at him. "Could have but didn't." Didn't Emeliano know he felt invincible?

"You need to think of the future, Cristiano. You and Valentino, why not go into business with your father? If

Pietro didn't already have three boys, I'd see if he'd take me on as partner," Emeliano said.

"Go to Rome, find a place and work up," Cristiano suggested, conscious of the attention from the woman at the next table. He didn't care if she eavesdropped. He had no secrets.

Except one.

"And my mother, what of her? You have it great, Cristiano."

He smiled, all for show. If only Emeliano knew the truth—all the truth—he'd look away in disgust. "How is your mother?"

"Ailing. Arthritis is a terrible thing." Emeliano flexed his hands. "I hope I never get it."

"Me, too."

Cristiano met the woman's gaze again when Emeliano left and didn't look away. She flushed slightly and looked at the baby, smiling at his babbling and arm waving. Covering one small fist with her hand, she leaned over to kiss him. Just then she glanced up again.

"I saw you on the Jet Ski," she said.

He nodded.

"You fell in the water."

"But I didn't fall."

She shrugged, glancing at the infant. Then looked shyly at him again. "It looked like great fun."

"It is. How old is your baby?" He looked at the child, trying to gauge if it were smaller than the one from last May. He wasn't often around infants and couldn't guess his age.

She smiled again, her eyes going all silvery. Nice combination of coloring. He wondered again who she was and why she was at Lake Clarissa.

"He's almost five months."

A boy. His father had two boys and a girl. Wait, make that four boys and a girl. He still couldn't get used to the startling fact his sister shared a few months ago—about two older half-brothers who were Americans. Too surreal. Another reason to keep away from his family. He wasn't sure how he felt about his father keeping that secret all his life.

The infant had dark hair and dark eyes. His chubby cheeks held no clue as to what he'd look like as an adult, but his coloring didn't match hers at all.

"Does he look like his father?"

"I have no idea. But his mother had dark eyes and hair. Maybe when he's older, I'll see some resemblance to the man who fathered him. Right now to me he looks like his mom." She reached out and brushed the baby's head in a light caress.

"He's not yours?"

She shook her head.

"A nanny?" So maybe there was no man in the picture. Was she watching the baby for a family? She seemed devoted to the child.

She shook her head again. "I'm his guardian. His mother died." She blinked back tears and Cristiano again felt that discomforting shift in his mid section. He hoped she wasn't going to cry. He never knew how to handle a woman in tears. He wanted to slay dragons or race away. Unfortunately he all too often had to comfort women—and men sometimes—in tears at their loss. He always did his best. Always felt it fell short.

Emeliano arrived with a tray laden with rigatoni, big salad and hot garlic bread. He glanced at the woman, then Cristiano. "Want to sit together?"

"No," Cristiano said.

At the same time she replied, "That would be fine, if he doesn't mind."

"Oops," she said immediately. "I guess you do mind." She put on a bright smile. "I'll be going soon."

He felt like a jerk. He hadn't meant to embarrass her. "Come, sit with me. I could use the company while I eat." He tried to make up for the faux pas, but she just gave a polite smile and said, "No, thanks anyway, I have to be going. This guy likes to ride in the stroller to see the sights." She fumbled for her wallet and began pulling out the euros to pay her bill.

Emeliano served Cristiano, gave him a wry look and hurried away to look after another customer.

By the high color in her cheeks, he knew she was embarrassed. They'd been talking; it seemed churlish to refuse when his friend made the suggestion. Now he wished he had waited a second, thought before he spoke.

She rose and gathered her purse and a diaper bag and quickly carried the baby to the front of the restaurant without looking at him again. There he saw the stroller he'd missed when he first entered. In a heartbeat, they were gone.

His sister would have scolded him for his bad manners. His father would have looked at him with sadness. Of course his father seemed perpetually sad since their mother had died so long ago. He'd never found another woman to share his life with.

Cristiano began to eat. The food was good, not excellent, but good. What did it matter? Seeing the baby reminded him of his friend Stephano's young daughter. Too young to have lost her father. Cristiano still couldn't believe his best friend had perished in the instant the second bomb had exploded. Many days he could almost believe he was on leave and would go back to work to find Stephano and the others on his squad ready to fight whatever fires came their way.

But his friend was gone. Forever.

Cristiano ate slowly, regretting his hasty refusal of sitting with the woman with the baby. Learning more about her would have kept his mind off his friend and his other worries.

Mariella bundled Dante up and placed him in the stroller. She couldn't get out of the restaurant fast enough. She felt the wave of embarrassment wash over her as she remembered offering to have the man sit at her table. He had definitely been annoyed. He probably had women falling over themselves to gain his attention with those dark compelling eyes and the tanned skin. He looked as if he brought the outdoors inside with him. He towered over the waiter. When he'd sat at the table next to hers she'd been impressed with his trim physique, wide shoulders and masculine air. He had such vitality around him.

She'd also been too flustered to ask the waiter if he'd ever seen Ariana in the restaurant. She'd even brought the picture of her friend to show around.

A moment later the thought popped into her head that the man talking to the waiter could even have been Dante's father. He had the dark eyes and hair for it.

"So who's your daddy, sweetie? Did he live around here or only bring your mother for a visit?" she asked the baby as they moved along the worn sidewalk. Shops enticed, but it was difficult to maneuver the stroller through the narrow aisles of the small stores. She needed a better plan to try to find Dante's father than simply showing Ariana's photograph to every man she saw and asking if he'd known her. Why ever would anyone admit to it if there'd been a problem with their relationship?

Stopping near the church, she sat on one of the wooden benches facing the town square. It was peaceful here.

Dressed warmly, she was comfortable on this sunny afternoon despite the cooler temperatures. Checking on Dante, she was pleased he was warm and animated, looking around at the different buildings, up at the leaves on the tree partially shading the bench.

"Tree," she said. She knew Dante probably couldn't care less what that was called as long as she fed him on time and kept him dry and warm.

She still felt stressed dealing with the baby and hoped this trip would not only help her find out more about his father, but bring them closer together, too. She'd read every book she could get her hands on about newborns, had enlisted the help of a couple of friends who had children. But nothing had prepared her for the task of being an instant mom twenty-four-seven. At least most mothers had months to get used to the idea. Plans and dreams—usually with a partner—centered on the new life arriving. Psyching themselves up for the challenges.

Instead, Dante had been Mariella's instant baby. She had known about him for less than a month before she became his mother. No warning, no preparation, and definitely no partner to share the task.

Dante was dozing when Mariella thought about returning to the cottage she'd rented. He'd sleep better in the crib she'd had set up for him. And she could finish unpacking and settle in. They'd be here a week so she needed to get organized, then she could decide how to go on.

"I didn't mean to run you off." She looked to her left and saw the man from the restaurant. He paused beside her. The sun glinted on his dark hair. His dark eyes looked straight into hers and caused her heart to bump up in rhythm. For a moment she couldn't breathe. She felt a flare of attraction sweep through her. It made her almost giddy. Certainly not the way a mother should react. She hadn't expected to see him again—especially so soon after the restaurant.

"I was ready to leave," she said. She looked away. He was gorgeous—tall, tanned and fit. Was he on holiday? Why else would he be Jet Skiing and then taking a long lunch in the middle of the week? Or did he live around here and have the kind of job that allowed mid-week excursions to the lake? She wanted to know more about him.

He sat beside her on the bench, staring at the fountain at the center of the square. She flicked him a glance, but he seemed oblivious, still focused on the fountain. She noted no rings on his hands. She looked where he looked. The honey-colored stone blended well with the mountain setting. The cobbled street gave testimony to the age of the village. Surely he'd seen it all before. As if reading her thoughts, he turned and looked at her, offering his hand.

"My name is Cristiano Casali. Emeliano's suggestion caught me by surprise. You have a baby and I thought it best—never mind. I apologize for my rudeness."

She shook his hand and then pulled hers free. Tingling from the brief contact, she cleared her throat and tried to concentrate on what he said and not on the amazing feelings suddenly pulsing through her. He was just a man being courteous.

"Not to worry. I'm Mariella Holmes." She didn't dare look at him. Let her get her roiling emotions under some control first.

"So the mystery of the baby intrigues me. And if you knew about how things have been with me lately, that's surprising. How is he yours? You look too young to be a guardian of anyone." He glanced at the baby, then back at her.

"I'm twenty-two and old enough. I have friends who didn't go to university who married young and already have two children." She would never confide to a stranger how unprepared she felt being a new mother. If she'd just had more time to prepare, maybe she'd feel better suited to the role.

"Okay, you're old enough, but how?"

"His mother died. Before she did, I agreed to be his guardian. Ariana had no other family." She was proud she could say her friend's name without bursting into tears. Studying him as she spoke, she saw no start of recognition when she said her friend's name.

"The father didn't object?" he asked.

"I don't have a clue who the father is." She'd asked as many of Ariana's friends as she knew if they had known the man. No one had. It was a secret her friend had taken with her.

Cristiano frowned at her statement. Mariella elaborated in a rush, feeling the need to explain.

"Dante's mother was my best friend, Ariana. She met some guy and fell in love. Apparently when she told him she was pregnant, the man abandoned her. I didn't know any of this. I was in New York when I got her phone call shortly before Dante was born. She was sick and asked me to come back to Italy. I did, instantly. When she asked me to take Dante, how could I refuse? We were as close as sisters, yet she never told me his father's name though I asked many times." She looked at the child, feeling the weight of her commitment heavy on her shoulders.

"What happened to your friend?" Cristiano asked gently.

Mariella took a moment to gather her composure. It was still hard to talk about the death of her very dearest and longest friend. "She died of leukemia. She found out she had it while pregnant and refused any treatment until after the baby was born. He arrived healthy and strong, though a couple of weeks early. She died when he was two weeks old."

Mariella tried to blot out the picture of her friend those last weeks. Her thin cheeks, lackluster hair, sad, sad eyes. Ariana had known she wouldn't live to see her baby grow up. She'd implored Mariella over and over to promise to raise Dante for her. The day the guardianship paper had been signed, Ariana had smiled for the last time and soon thereafter slipped into a coma, which led to her death.

"You still seem awfully young to be tied down with a baby. Shouldn't you be out enjoying life at this stage?"

"Thanks for your concern, but I'm fine with being Dante's guardian." She didn't need some stranger questioning her ability to watch the baby. It was a huge responsibility, Mariella knew that already. And she often questioned her ability herself when lying awake at night, trying to anticipate all she needed to do to raise Dante. Mariella considered it an honor to be chosen to raise her friend's baby.

No one needed to know how overwhelmed she felt. And how while she loved Dante, it was not the deep maternal love she knew other mothers felt immediately for their child. Mariella loved this baby, but couldn't help feeling a bit cheated of her best friend. If Ariana had not been pregnant when she'd found out about the leukemia, she might be alive today. Mariella felt alone in a way she'd never experienced before; isolated even more by the demands of an infant.

Not that she'd tell anyone in a million years. What if it ever came back to Dante? She did love him. She did! But she had loved her friend for far longer.

"I need to go," she said, jumping up. She had to escape her thoughts. She could do this. She would do this. Or find his father and make sure Dante had a loving family to welcome him.

"Seems like I run you off at every turn," Cristiano said.

She started pushing the stroller. Cristiano rose and fell into step beside her. "Why are you here at this time of year? Most tourists come in the summer months, when they can use the lake," he said. Glancing at the baby, he added, "And they come when their kids are older and can play by the water. We'll be getting rain before long. It's already colder now than a couple of weeks ago. Not very conducive to sitting by the lake."

"I thought maybe I could find out about Dante's father. But now that I'm here, I'm not so sure." It had been a foolish thought. Clutching at straws, that was what. The man could have brought her friend here for a get-away weekend. She only knew Ariana had been happy at Lake Clarissa.

"What do you know about him?" Cristiano asked.

"Nothing. Ariana wouldn't talk about him at all."

They approached the small resort on the lake. Traffic was light on the street. The quiet of the afternoon was interrupted only by birdsong.

"You have the last cottage, right?"

"How did you know that?" Mariella asked, looking at him. He had obviously shortened his stride to stay even with her. She wondered if he'd come to the cottage and stay a while. She'd love to put the baby down and have some adult conversation—especially with a man so unlike others she knew.

"I saw it was occupied when I was skiing."

"Do you live here year round?" she asked.

"No." With that one word, he changed. She glanced at him, but his expression gave nothing away. He looked ahead as they walked, not elaborating on the single-word response. But she could feel the difference, the way he closed himself off. A bleakness in his eyes that hadn't been there before. What had she said?

"Visiting?" she probed. He'd asked enough questions, she could ask a few. Her curiosity grew. If Ariana had been around, she'd have called her up to tell her about the daredevil and how he was a poster child for sexy, virile Italian male. And speculate why he was at Lake Clarissa and discuss ways she might get to know him better.

"Staying a while," was all he said.

Her curiosity arose another notch. But she didn't know him well enough to pester with a lot of questions. Though a dozen burned on her tongue.

The path to the cottage was packed dirt lined with rocks. Bumpy and uneven. It was a bit of a struggle for Mariella to push the stroller, but Dante loved being bounced around. He gurgled and looked enchanted with the bouncy ride.

"Here, let me," Cristiano said at one point, reaching out to take the stroller. His hand brushed hers as he reached for the handle and she folded her arms across her chest, savoring the tingling. Walking beside him made her feel sheltered and feminine. This was how a family should be, father, mother and baby. She blinked. No going off in day-dreams, she admonished.

"Thanks," she said when they reached the fifth cabin. The trees shaded in the afternoon. The small stone terrace had two chairs and a small table to use when sitting to watch the lake.

The wind had picked up a bit and it was definitely cooler than before.

"I can manage from here," she said with a smile. "I hope I see you in town again," she said, feeling daring. It would be too awful to have this be their sole encounter.

He stepped away from the stroller and looked at her.

Mariella had the feeling he wanted to say something. His eyes seemed full of turmoil. But he merely nodded and said, "Maybe you will. I come to town often. Goodbye."

She watched as he walked back along the path, his long legs covering the distance in a short time. One minute he was there, the next gone. And he took some of the brightness of the day with him.

She should have shown him the picture. Maybe he had seen Ariana. Where did he live? Why had her question caused the change? One minute he seemed open and friendly, the next closed and reserved. Not that it was any of her business. But she couldn't help the curiosity. Was he married? Separated or divorced?

She hoped she saw him again before she left.

Cristiano walked back to the square wondering if he was losing his mind. It had been months since anything had caught his attention as strongly as Mariella Holmes had. She was pretty—granted. But he'd seen other pretty women.

But not like her, something inside whispered. Her hair had that healthy glossy sheen that caught the light and reflected golden highlights. It looked thick and silky. He wished he could have touched it to verify the satiny feel. Her eyes were clear and honest. Her emotions shone through as they changed from steel grey to silvery.

He tried to ignore the image of her that kept flashing in his mind. Her gentle touch with the baby, her bright smile. The way she had of brushing back her hair when the breeze blew it in her face. Was he ready to risk a normal life now? Had things finally turned for the better? He had too much baggage to think of getting involved.

Yet she also came with baggage—a baby.

He'd never envisioned himself as a father. Or even a husband. He liked speed, challenges, adrenaline-producing activities that confirmed over and over he was alive and living life to the fullest. His job as a firefighter was exhilarating, but dangerous. Other men on his crew were married, but he'd never felt it fair to constantly risk his life if someone was depending on him.

He stopped along the sidewalk and gazed over the water. He knew he might never join his crew in battling a blaze again, or, then again, he might be fit to return to duty next week. No one knew what the future held. Maybe his held a silvery-eyed beauty. But he knew he had better be damned sure before going down that path.

Mariella Holmes had domesticity written all over her. She was not for a holiday romance. It'd be best for both their sakes to stay away from her.

Reaching the motorcycle, he sat on it a moment, watching neighbors and townspeople going about their business, shopping, greeting each other. Some waved to him and he acknowledged the greetings. Did they have secrets that would change lives? Did they have families who had kept secrets that were now coming out? Did they have sorrows and loss like those that had dimmed Mariella's smile?

Too philosophical for him. He put on the black helmet and started the bike. It was a short drive from the village of Lake Clarissa to the family cottage. He had liked being able to walk to the lake as a child. The happy times their family had once had seemed far away these days. Passing the driveway, he continued on, revving up his speed as if he could outrun the memories on the deserted mountain roads.

It was after dark when he pulled to a stop at the back of the family cottage. His excessive speed would give his father a heart attack. The harrowing hairpin turns provided a challenge he loved meeting. The fabulous scenery that raced by was a strong contrast to the smoke and dust and hell of his last weeks in Rome. He much preferred the vistas the hills offered to the memory of death and destruction and loss.

He entered the kitchen and ignored the dishes on the counter and in the sink. Going straight to the cabinet near the stove, he opened it and took down the bottle of brandy. It was far lighter than it had been last night. Not enough, now, to get rip-roaring drunk. He set it on the counter, reached for a glass, then stared at the bottle for a long moment. With a violent smash of his hand he knocked it on the stone floor where it broke into a thousand pieces, the smell of brandy filling the air.

He didn't need the stupor drink caused. Striding to his room, he stripped and went to take a shower, thinking of the bright smile on Mariella Holmes' face, and the love she showered on the baby. That was what he wanted. To feel connected. To feel passion and caring and hope for the future. To love. Dared he risk seeing her again?

# CHAPTER TWO

MARIELLA rose at five to feed Dante. When he fell back asleep, she powered up her laptop and checked in on her clients, glad the rental cottage had Internet access. Working as a virtual assistant ensured she could work from home and at the hours that suited Dante's schedule. It was, however, a far cry from the work she'd thought she'd be doing after graduating from university.

She had often talked with friends in New York about setting up their own marketing firm. About setting New York on fire with their brilliant ideas and strong drive and determination. They'd fantasized about clients who would skyrocket them to the top of their field due to their impressive marketing.

Instead, she was quietly typing out another letter for a client miles away from the future she'd once envisioned. Yet she was grateful she'd found something that paid enough for their small flat and all their other needs. A baby was expensive. She could have been in worse shape.

By the time Dante woke from his nap in the late morning, Mariella had caught up on everything and had shut down her computer. Two of her major clients were away this week, which had freed enough time to allow her to start her search for Dante's father. It was a haphazard way to search for someone, but it was all she had to start with. Hiring someone would prove too expensive.

Bathing the baby when he awoke, then taking a quick shower after he'd been fed, she quickly prepared a light lunch. He was still awake and the day was lovely, so she took him in the stroller to the patio. Sitting on the wooden bench, she wished the cottage had come with a rocking chair. She had purchased one as soon as she'd known she would have Dante. It was soothing to rock the baby as he drank his bottle. Still, they'd only be here a week.

No daring Jet Ski riding today, she noticed. Or had Cristiano gone out earlier that morning and she'd missed him? She might have been busy with her work, but surely she would have heard the Jet Ski? She tried to ignore the pang of disappointment. She gazed at the deep blue of the water and the lighter blue of the sky. Contrasting with the dark green of the evergreen trees, it was an idyllic setting. She felt her heart lighten a bit. On impulse, she reached for the baby and held him sitting up in her arms as she absorbed the tranquility.

"Isn't this a pretty place?" she said, kissing the plump cheek. Dante gazed at her with wide brown eyes. Her heart expanded with love for her friend's child. He was such a precious little boy.

"Oh, Dante, what are we going to do?" she whispered. "I love you to bits, but I wish every time I see you that your mamma could see you. She loved you so much. One day I'll tell you just how much."

Then a noise caught her attention and she looked at the lake, almost grinning in surprised recognition. "It's him," she told the baby. "The man we met yesterday. Only you slept through most of it."

Cristiano sped across the water at a daring rate. She

watched, mesmerized. Did the man have no fear? She knew she'd be terrified to go at such speeds across the water.

He made it seem effortless. He and the machine seemed to be one as he banked and flew even faster toward the far shore. Soon she couldn't see him, only the arcing plume from the power ski. A moment later she saw the turn and then he was racing toward them. She stood, carried the baby to the edge of the patio and turned so Dante could also see the water. She had no idea if he was watching the Jet Ski, but she could scarcely take her eyes off the man riding. She remembered every inch of him—tall, tanned skin, dark hair shaggy and long. Remembering his dark eyes that had gazed into hers so intently had her heart racing.

She'd hoped to see him again. Wanted to learn more about him. Hear him tell about the village and the people who lived here. And tell her what he did in life, where he lived, what made him laugh. Was there a special woman in his life? She didn't think so, but would like to know for sure.

Was there any place in his life for her?

Foolish thoughts. She was only here for a short time.

As he approached the small dock in front of her cottage, he slowed, coming to a coasting stop as he cut the engine and glided to the wooden planks. Bumping slightly, he sat back and looked up at her.

She almost laughed in delight and, holding Dante firmly, she carefully followed the path to the dock, walking out the few steps to where he bobbed in the water.

"Hi," she said. "That looks amazing. How fast do you go?" She couldn't help her grin as she took in the broad shoulders, the muscular legs straddling the machine. For a moment she wished she'd checked her hair before coming out. But with the breeze, it would be windblown no matter what. Cristiano looked fantastic, tousled hair, ruddy cheeks, and those compelling brown eyes that about melted her heart.

"Not too fast. Want to go for a spin?" he asked with a cheeky grin, taking in the baby.

She laughed and shook her head, jiggling Dante a little. "Not with a baby, thank you very much. I'd never let him go on one of those."

"Maybe when he's older," Cristiano said, sitting casually on the floating machine, one foot on the dock anchoring him in place.

She eyed the machine with some wariness. "Too dangerous. Aren't you cold?" The breeze reminded her it was fall, no hot summer days to be refreshed by the water. With his dark eyes focused on her, she felt her temperature rise. The attraction that flared between them confused her. She'd never felt emotions like this with other men she'd known. Was Cristiano different in some way? Or was it just normal reaction after months of only dealing with Dante?

"My feet are freezing. I'm ready to head back. You going into the village today?"

Mariella hadn't been sure before, but this clinched it. "Yes. We'll be walking over in a little while. Are you planning to be there?" She gave him her best smile. Was she flirting with the man? Yes—and it felt great.

"I'll buy you an ice-cream cone." His eyes locked with hers, as if urging her to say yes.

She felt daring and excited at the same time. She nodded. "I'd like that." Trying to subdue the excitement from her voice, she said, "Don't fall in on your way back."

"No chance." He pushed off and in a moment the motor caught and he headed the short distance to the town's small marina.

She watched until she couldn't see him clearly.

"So, we've been invited to see him again," she said to Dante, hurrying back to the cottage to get the stroller. She could hardly wait.

Cristiano ran the Jet Ski up on the floating berth and turned off the motor. He'd left his clothes on the motorcycle again only this time didn't just pull them over his wet ones, but used the men's facilities at the public boathouse to change. He refused to examine closely why he'd stopped by the cottage to see her. He'd spotted her on the patio and impulse had driven him closer.

The only way to know if she was around, without being totally blatant about it, was to use the lake. When he'd seen her on the porch, the lure of the Jet Ski had vanished. He'd wanted to see her again.

Dressed, he bundled the wet clothes, strapping them on the back of the motorcycle. It would be a two-minute ride to the square. He had no idea if she'd already arrived. Maybe he should have gone home to get the car.

She was talking with the priest in front of the church when Cristiano entered the square. Stopping some distance away, he cut the engine and sat on the motorcycle as he watched, curious what she could be talking to Father Andreas about. The old man shook his head and then smiled down at the baby in the stroller.

In an instant the sunshine dimmed. Cristiano remembered the feel of the baby in the cradle of his arm, the small, terrified child clutched with the other. The baby cried and cried. The nightmare of smoke and darkness and wailing screams filled his senses. For a moment he was there, back in the tunnels of the metro, fighting for breath, for a foothold, for life itself with two children who were too young to die.

He could feel the heat of the fire behind him. Hear the shouts of other first responders, everyone trying to fight their way through hell. Screams of the dying, distorted shadows as the flames flared and waned. He could smell the smoke and dust as clearly as he had when his helmet shattered.

He couldn't breathe. He couldn't see. Which way was out? Which way lay sunshine and fresh air and life itself?

A shout sounded louder than the rest. Something bounced on his thigh and Cristiano blinked, looking down at the rubber ball that rolled away from where it had struck him. Two boys raced after it, their laughter and shouts echoing in the square.

He looked around. Mariella was pushing the stroller toward him. The priest was standing on the stairs leading into the old church smiling at the children who played around the fountain. The sun shone in a cloudless sky. A pastoral scene, one of peace and tranquility and the very fabric of life.

Taking a breath, he hoped he could keep his mind in the present. He'd thought he had these flashbacks under control. It had been days since—

"Hello,' she said as she approached, that wide smile holding his gaze.

No one seemed to notice anything out of the ordinary. Only Cristiano knew he'd had another flashback—thankfully brief this time. He never knew when they'd come, how debilitating they'd be. This one had passed quickly. Because of Mariella?

He didn't want her to know. They'd spend some time together today, enjoy each other's company and then he'd take off for the cottage, the bolt-hole he'd claimed when he had been released from the hospital. No one in his family had known he'd been injured far beyond the ankle that had broken.

"Are you all right?" Mariella asked when she reached the motorcycle, a questioning look in her eyes.

"Sure." He needed to change that subject quickly. "How do you know Father Andreas?"

"We just met. He was walking by and I showed him my friend's picture to see if he recognized her. He didn't."

She drew it from her pocket and held it out to Cristiano. He took it. The laughing expression on the unknown woman's face tugged at his heart. This was the young mother who had died. She didn't look as old as Mariella. Did Mariella feel the same tearing grief he felt whenever he thought about his friend Stephano? Did she regret time wasted when, if she had only known the future, she would have changed what she did in the weeks, days left before her friend's death?

Had he known Stephano would die in the bomb explosion last May, would he have done more in the days leading to that fateful time? Or would he have taken everything for granted as he had expecting them both to live forever?

It was a lesson well learned. No one could predict the future. Enjoy life while he could. As long as he could.

Handing it back, he said, "I don't recognize her. When was she here?"

"I don't know. Sometime within the last eighteen months is all I have. I thought at restaurants or shops someone would recognize her." She slipped the photograph back into her pocket and shrugged. "So far no one has."

"What are you going to do if you find him?"

"I'm still not sure. A baby should have his family around him. I'm hoping the father comes from a large family who would love Dante. I may never find him. But I want to tell Dante when he's older that I tried."

"Let your family be his."

She shrugged. "I have no family. Ariana was the closest thing to a sister I had. Both our parents are dead. Neither of us had any other living relatives. Maybe it's foolish to search for his father, but if it were me, I'd want to know. Easier maybe to find out about him now than when Dante is twenty-one."

Cristiano didn't know how he'd feel about finding out he had a child at some future date, after the child was grown. Had the man truly not wanted any connection, or had his initial reaction been panic that he now regretted?

In a way, his family's recent events paralleled Mariella's situation. He still didn't know how to deal with the newly acquired knowledge that his father had other sons, older than he was. They'd grown up a world apart. Would there be some connection should they ever meet? Would blood call to blood? Or would they forever be strangers?

Cristiano could never knowingly give up a child if he had one. How had his father done it?

He kicked down the stand and got off the motorcycle. "Have you questioned everyone in town?"

"So far only the priest and the proprietor at the resort."

"Come, I'll buy you an ice-cream cone and you can ask there. Seems to me your best bet would be restaurants and shops where visitors are likely to go."

"Maybe, but they could have simply come for a weekend at the height of the season when she'd have been just one of many," she said, pushing the stroller ahead as they walked around the square. The sun shone in a cloudless sky. The air was cool, but comfortable. And she was walking beside a handsome, attentive man. She didn't want to talk about Ariana and her lost love. She wanted to learn more about Cristiano.

The ice-cream shop was virtually empty.

"Not the time of year for ice cream. Want something else?" he asked.

"No. This will be good. I can give Dante a tiny taste. He's not eating real food yet."

They ordered, then went back into the square to sit on a bench in the sunshine.

"Did you once live here? The proprietress knew you," she asked.

"My grandparents were from Lake Clarissa. They had a small cottage nearby. We lived with them when we were children and papa was busy working. Summer days we would swim in the lake. Sometimes we'd camp out overnight in the forest."

He watched as Mariella licked her ice cream. The lonely existence he'd chosen these past few months melted away. He hadn't felt normal for a long time. What was it about this woman that changed that? He could forget the horror that haunted him when he was around her. Maybe he should take her home with him and keep her with him until the spell was broken.

Yet moments before he'd had another flashback. He looked away. He had no business coming to town. What if he had a major meltdown? He had to beat this thing before he could get his life back.

"Sounds like you had a lot of fun here," she said.

"Yes, we did, it was a happy time. My grandfather lived until I was almost an adult. He continued to live here even when we had all moved away from home, he was a part of the place. He gave our childhood an extra sense of fun and excitement, beyond playing in the forest or at the lake." Hard to think about the past when he listened to her voice, soft and lilting.

"Is that where you got your daredevil ways?" she asked with a teasing grin.

"Daredevil ways?" That grin felt like a kick to the mid section. For a moment he forgot where they were and wondered what she'd do if he leaned over and kissed her. Her eyes sparkled, there were freckles scattered across her nose, kisses from the sun. He looked away before he did something foolish, such as trail kisses over every one. They'd just met. It was too early to think about kisses.

Yet as the seconds ticked by, the thought would not fade. He'd like to take her hand and feel the soft warmth against his palm. Sit closer so he could feel every radiant bit of heat from her body. Lean in so she could only see him. Find out what fascinated him about her.

"Racing across the lake like you were trying to fly. I consider that amazingly like a daredevil," she explained, leaning closer.

Did she feel that same pull of attraction? He took a breath, taking in the scent of her, light and flowery. He held his breath for a moment to savor it. Then released it and shook his head. "I'm no daredevil. You should meet my brother Valentino. Now, he's the daredevil in the family. Today was just Jet Skiing."

She pointed to the motorcycle across the square. "That's a dangerous mode of transportation."

"Not if you know what you're doing. It's like flying along the road."

"So tell me about living here, especially during summer," she invited as they ate their cones.

Cristiano didn't want to talk about himself; he wanted to know more about Mariella. But if he offered something, he could have her reciprocate. He began recounting summer days playing at the edge of the lake, climbing around on the rocky shore and learning to swim. Then the nights he and Valentino had spent roaming the woods, feeling daring and grown up braving the darkness.

She laughed at his stories and from time to time admonished Dante to stop listening, she didn't want him to get ideas. The longer Cristiano talked, the lighter the world seemed to grow. He liked hearing her laugh. The more she did, the more outrageous he made the stories.

"Now, tell me about your summer holidays," he said when he'd wound down. They'd long since finished their ice cream. The baby had fallen asleep and Mariella seemed content to sit in the sunshine. It was as if she brought sunshine into his life where only darkness had once dwelt.

"We always went to places to learn more about history. My father was an accountant, but he loved history. So we visited Pompeii and Turin, Florence, of course, and Venice." She smiled in memory and Cristiano knew from her expression how much she'd enjoyed those vacations with her parents.

"Ariana went with us when we were teenagers. We flirted like crazy with the gondoliers in Venice. Of course they ignored us." She laughed, then her eyes unexpectedly filled with tears. "We should have had the chance to remember all those foolish activities when we were old with grandchildren running around. It's so unfair she died."

Cristiano wanted to comfort her, but only time would completely heal the pain.

"I had a friend who died last May. Life is unfair. I'm single with few responsibilities. He had a wife and two children. Why him? It should have been me."

She looked at him in shock. "Never say that. Who knows why some die young? But I have never thought it should have been me instead of Ariana. Life is too precious. We need to enjoy every moment. Maybe even more so because in a way we are now living also for our friends, experiencing life as they will no longer be able to."

The memories were threatening again. The fear he'd end up hiding beneath the bench they now sat on in the middle of the day, yelling for Stephano, was real. He had to get away before he cracked.

He stood. "I have to go.' The tightness in his chest grew. It was becoming more difficult to breathe. He held onto the present desperately.

"Thank you for the ice cream. And the conversation," she said.

He nodded and strode to the motorcycle. Staying any longer was flirting with danger. He knew his limits—and he'd passed them already. Time to get away.

He started the bike and looked over at Mariella. She was watching him, her head tilted slightly as if wondering what had gone wrong. If she only knew all that was wrong.

"Come tomorrow," he said.

She smiled and nodded.

Mariella watched Cristiano leave. He was the most perplexing man she'd ever met. She'd thought they'd been having a great conversation when he'd abruptly jumped up and left. She tried to remember what she could have said to cause such a reaction. They'd been exchanging memories and she had lamented the fact she and Ariana wouldn't grow old together.

So who was his friend who had died young? Such an odd thing for them to have in common, yet for a moment it brought her comfort. He was someone who could understand the sadness she felt for the loss of her friend.

The evening was quiet. Mariella played with Dante until the baby fell asleep. She liked this impromptu vacation. She was still working the odd hours to keep her clients happy. But she had more time to spend with the baby. And with several months' of experience behind her, she was growing more confident in her abilities than that first month as a stunned guardian with a tiny infant and no job.

She could not afford to stay in Lake Clarissa for long, however. She wanted to expand the search for Dante's father before she had to return to Rome. Stopping in a few shops, speaking with the priest didn't encompass all of the village. Tomorrow she'd make a concerted effort to visit more places. Then if she had no results, the next day she'd move on to Monta Correnti.

After the baby was asleep, she checked her laptop for any new assignments, then surfed the Net. She put in Cristiano's name on a whim and was startled when pages loaded. He was a firefighter. He'd been a first responder to the bombing in Rome last May. She read the compelling newspaper articles. The man was a hero. He'd gone down into the bombing scene time and again. He'd saved seven lives, become injured himself and still fought to bring a baby and small child through the smoke-filled metro tunnel to safety that last trip.

Wow. She read every article she could on the bombing. She'd been finishing up finals in New York when the terrorist attack had hit Rome. Once she'd been assured none of her friends had been injured, she'd relegated it and all other news to the back of her mind as she madly studied. Even if she'd seen Cristiano's name back then, she never would have remembered it.

She had suspected he had some physically demanding job. He was strong, muscular and fit. He moved with casual grace in that tall body. And being around him gave her a definite sense of security. She searched further hoping for a picture, but the only ones she saw were of firefighters and police in uniform, battling for people's lives.

It was late when she shut down the computer. Checking the doors and windows before retiring, she realized how much it had cooled down in the cottage. She switched on the wall heater and went to get ready for bed. Dante was fast asleep in one of the fleecy sleepers she used for him at night. She covered him with a light blanket and shivered; her fingers were freezing. Fall had truly arrived. At least the baby would be warm through the night, and once she was beneath the blankets she'd be toasty warm herself.

Cristiano sat upright with a bolt. He became instantly awake, breathing hard, the terror still clinging from the nightmare. He took deep gulps of breath, trying to still his racing heart. It was pitch dark—not unlike the tunnel after the bombing. Only the lights from their helmets had given any illumination in the dusty and smoky world.

He threw off the blanket and rose, walking to the window and opening it wide for the fresh air. The cold breeze swept over him, jarring him further. He breathed in the crisp air, relishing the icy clean feel. No smoke. No voices screaming in terror. Nothing here but the peaceful countryside in the middle of the night. The trees blotted out a lot of the stars. The moon rode low on the horizon, its light dancing on the shimmering surface of the lake, a sliver of which was visible from the window.

He gripped the sill and fought the remnants of the nightmare. It was hauntingly familiar. He'd had it often enough since that fateful day. Gradually the echoes of frantic screams faded. The horror receded. The soft normal sounds of night crept in.

Long moments later he turned to get dressed. There would be no more sleep tonight.

Once warmly clothed, he went to the motorcycle and climbed on board. A ride through the higher mountain roads would get him focused. He knew he was trying to outrun the demons. Nothing would ever erase that day from his mind. But he couldn't stay inside a moment longer. The wind rushed through his hair; the sting of cold air on his cheeks proved he was alive. And the lack of smoke was life-affirming. It was pure nectar after the hell he'd lived through.

Driving on the curving roads required skill and concentration. One careless moment and he could go spinning over the side and fall a hundred feet. The hills were deserted. No homes were back here, no one to see him as he made the tight turns, forcing the motorcycle to greater speed. He still felt that flare of exhilaration of conquering the challenge, his skills coming into play. At least he had this.

It was close to dawn when Cristiano approached the village. He'd made a wide circle and was heading back to home. A hot cup of espresso sounded good right about now.

He settled in on the road that curved around the lake. Soon he'd turn for the short climb to the family cottage. Then he smelt it.

Smoke.

His gut clenched. For a moment he thought he imagined it. He drew in a deep breath—it was in the air. Where there was smoke, there was fire. He slowed down and peered around. No one would have a campfire going at this hour; it was getting close to dawn. There, stronger now. To the left, near the lake.

For a moment indecision gripped him. Each breath identified the smoke as it wafted on the morning air. Forest fire? Building fire? He stopped the motorcycle, holding it upright with one foot on the ground. Every muscle tightened. He couldn't move. He felt paralyzed. Where were the village's firefighters? Why wasn't someone responding? Had the alarm even been sounded?

Seconds sped by.

Instinct kicked in. He slowly started moving, lifting his foot from the ground as the bike picked up speed.

He spotted a flicker of light where only darkness should be. He opened the throttle and raced toward the spot. In a moment, he recognized where he was—near the Bertatalis' row of cottages beside the lake. The flickering light came from the last one—the one Mariella and the baby were in!

He gunned the motor and leaned on the horn. In only a moment, lights went on in the Bertatalis' main house. He didn't stop, hoping they'd see the fire and respond. Seconds counted. Smoke inhalation could be fatal long before the actual flames touched anyone. Stopping near the cottage, he threw down the bike and raced to the door. He could see the fire through the living-room window almost consuming the entire area. The roof was already burning with flames escaping into the night. It would be fatal to enter that room.

Running to the back, he tried to figure out which window was the bedroom. Pounding on the glass, he heard no response. He hit his fist against the glass, but nothing happened. Quickly looked for anything to help; there—a large branch of a tree had fallen. Praying the baby was not sleeping beneath the window, he swung it like a bat, shattering the glass.

Smoke poured out. He could see the flames eagerly devouring the living room through the open bedroom door.

"Mariella," he shouted, levering himself up on the sill, brushing away glass shards, feeling the slight prick of a cut. He coughed in the smoky air.

"Huh?"

The sleepy voice responded. He jumped into the room and quickly assessed the situation. The door was open, the flames visible through the roiling smoke. Time was of the essence.

"Get up," he yelled, slamming shut the bedroom door, hoping it would hold the flames until he could get them out of the room. Where was Dante? He searched for the baby by touch in the smoke-filled room. There, near the wall, a cry sounded. He snatched up Dante and looked for Mariella. She was not responding. Had she already been overcome by smoke?

Stepping quickly as the crackling sounded louder, he found her still in bed and dragged her up.

"The cottage is on fire," he said as calmly as he could, trying to get through to her. He heard the sirens. Finally. Fear closed his throat as he looked overhead. An explosion paralyzed him. Was the tunnel caving in? Were there more bombs? Why wasn't his breathing mask working? He coughed in the smoke and moved toward the opening, pulling her with him. Echoes of men and women's screams sounded. The baby began screaming. Where was the little boy? Where was Stephano? Who could have done such a thing? How long did they have until everyone was safe?

"Cristiano?" Mariella's voice broke through. She coughed as she stumbled beside him. "What happened?"

"Don't know. Get out." They had reached the window and he scooped her up until she had her feet out the window, then pushed her gently until she jumped free. One leg over the sill, Dante in his arms, he didn't hesitate. A bright show of sparks and fire exploded as part of the front roof collapsed. Jumping free, he grabbed her arm and pulled her away from the cottage, the baby wailing in his arms. Past and present merged. Cristiano didn't stop running until he recognized the lake. Mariella kept up with him, coughing in the cold air.

The village volunteer firefighters were on their way. The sirens pierced the dawn air. Cristiano fought to keep his mind focused on the present, to be by the lake, to ignore the clamoring of his mind to relive the terror of a day in May.

In only moments the fire engine stopped, men scrambling to positions. Leaning against a tree, Cristiano stared at the fire, his throat tight. Tonight had not ended in tragedy.

"All my things," Mariella said, watching as the bedroom seemed to blossom with fire. "My laptop, my clothes. Dante's clothes. How could this happen?" She had tears running down her face. A moment later she was coughing again, shivering in the dawn light.

He pulled her closer, his arm around her shoulder, the baby screaming in his arms. "They are only things. You and the baby are safe, that's what's important." He offered up a quick prayer that he'd been able to save them. He'd faced his worst fear and come through.

Stephano and so many others hadn't been as lucky.

He watched the fire devour the cottage. In only moments it was completely engulfed in flames. He could feel the heat from where they stood.

She shivered again and he looked at her. The fire gave plenty of illumination. Shrugging out of his jacket, he wrapped it around her and handed her the crying baby. Her feet were still bare and must be freezing in the cold. Without a word, he picked them both up and headed toward the Bertatalis' main house. His ankle felt stiff, but it held. With grim satisfaction for the healing his body had done, he stepped carefully on the uneven ground, swinging wide around the burning cottage.

She coughed and tried to comfort the crying baby.

Signora Bertatali stood on the porch of her home, tears running down her cheek. When she saw Cristiano carrying Mariella and the baby, she hurried over.

"Thank God they are safe. Cristiano, thank you. Let me take the baby," she said, reaching out for Dante. "What happened?"

"I don't know," he said. "I saw the fire from the road and came to get them."

Mariella flung one arm around his neck. "I was asleep. Cristiano woke me up. How could the fire start?" She coughed again so hard, he almost dropped her.

"Try to take a deep slow breath. You're suffering from smoke inhalation."

"I don't know how this could happen. Oh, my dear, when I realized it was our cottage I feared the worst. Paolo has gone to help the firefighters. We'll know more after they tell us. Come, inside where it's warm. Did you leave the stove on or something?" Signora Bertatali asked, leading the way to her home. The warmth after the cold dawn felt wonderful. The baby stopped crying when in the light, blinking around, still looking as if he'd begin again in an instant.

"No. I turned it off after dinner," Mariella said.

"Oh, your poor feet. They're cut. Let me get some cloths and towels and take care of that," Signora Bertatali exclaimed, hurrying into the back bathroom, still jiggling the baby, trying to comfort him.

"I had to break a window to get into the bedroom. The living room was engulfed with flames when I arrived," Cristiano said, lowering Mariella down on a chair and kneeling in front of her to examine her feet as she began coughing again. She drew his jacket closer. A deep cut with a glass shard still in her left foot was bleeding; there were minor cuts on her right foot that had already stopped.

"This looks as if it needs stitches," he said, taking one of the towels Signora Bertatali brought and, after pulling the glass out, wrapped her foot.

The next while was chaotic. More volunteers arrived. Then the ambulance from Monta Correnti. Mariella and Dante were loaded up and taken to hospital while Cristiano stayed behind.

"I'll come to the hospital soon," he said as they drove away.

Now that the situation was under control, he watched from a distance until the fire was out. The adrenalin was wearing off. He could hear Stephano calling him. Feel the darkness closing in even as the sun broke on the horizon.

Retrieving his motorcycle, he roared off once more—trying to outrace the past.

# CHAPTER THREE

MARIELLA braced herself against another bump as the ambulance sped toward the hospital. Dante cried until she picked him up to cuddle, trying to hold him around the oxygen nodules they both wore. He grew quiet at that and snuggled against Mariella. "Oh, sweet thing, we almost died." Tears pricked her eyes. She caught a sob. How could the cottage catch fire? And why had there been no alarms to alert them of the danger before it was too late? The first she'd known of the emergency was when she heard Cristiano calling her name. Smoke had filled their room and she'd almost passed out trying to get out of bed and to safety. Breathing had been almost impossible.

The next thing she remembered was stumbling into the yard with Cristiano while Dante cried. Thank God he was safe. They both were.

Her head pounded and her eyes watered again. Coughing, she felt she could not draw a full breath. A weight seemed pressed against her chest.

"We'll have you to hospital in just a short while. They'll bathe your eyes and continue the oxygen until morning," the EMT said, handing her a tissue to wipe the tears.

The baby had settled down, looked as if he was going back to sleep. She kissed his cheek, so grateful. Mariella wished she could drop off as he did and forget everything—if only for a few hours. Who would think such things happened while on holiday?

Once they reached the hospital, nurses swarmed around the ambulance. One gently took the baby, promising to take good care of him as she whisked him away to be seen by a doctor. Another helped Mariella into a wheelchair and pushed her quickly into the ER. It was quiet except for the two of them. In a short while a doctor had cleaned the cuts and stitched up the one on her left foot.

"Where's my baby?" she asked.

"He's in Pediatrics, on oxygen. A pediatrician has checked him out. Except for smoke inhalation, he seems fine. You can see him soon."

Mariella nodded. She already missed him. She needed to see again that he was all right. But patience was called for. For the first time she had a moment to think. Cristiano had saved them. She had no idea how he'd happened to be there, but she thanked God he had been. He was a hero. Without his intervention, she and Dante could have died.

After she'd been seen by the doctor, she was conveyed to a semi-private room by way of the pediatric ward. Once satisfied Dante was safely asleep, she allowed herself to be taken to her own room where she insisted she could bathe herself. After a quick shower, she gladly lay down, with oxygen, and tried to sleep—but the horrors of the night haunted her. What if Cristiano hadn't arrived? She and the baby could have been burned to death. What had caused the fire? What had brought Cristiano there at exactly the right time? It was much, much later before she fell into a fitful sleep.

Mariella stood by the window of the hospital room in the late morning gazing at the beauty before her. The gardens of the hospital gave way to the view of rolling hills that gave this area so much of its beauty. She knew the lake lay beyond her view. From her vantage point she saw only the edge of a bustling town and the distant serene countryside. The village was hidden behind a fold in the hills and no trace of smoke marred the crystal-blue sky.

Everyone went along with their daily lives. She had lost clothes and her laptop. And her photo of Ariana. Dante had only the sleeper he wore when they were rescued. Her livelihood depended on connections with her clients. She had to get another computer soon. She had backup files at home, so wouldn't totally start from the beginning. But this would certainly put a crimp in things.

The few hours' sleep she'd managed made her feel refreshed. She needed her wits about her to get back on track. Maybe she should consider returning to Rome immediately. But she wasn't sure when she'd have another break in her workload to look for Dante's father. If she didn't do some checking now, people would forget. Maybe they already had. But she owed it to the baby to find out anything she was able to.

Even with oxygen she still used she felt as though her lungs were on fire and it was difficult to breathe. Still, things were improving—she could go several minutes without the racking coughs.

She was declared healthy enough to be discharged, with a follow-up visit scheduled for a few days later.

She hurried to the pediatric ward, limping slightly because of the stitches in her left foot. She slowed in surprise to see Cristiano staring at the babies in the nursery.

"Cristiano?"

He turned and smiled when he saw her, giving her a critical look. "How are you today?"

She coughed, then smiled as she came up to him. "Much better. Doctor said I can go home and come back in a few days for another checkup." She looked into the nursery. "Is Dante in there?"

"No, these are newborns. Look how small they are."

She noticed the four babies and smiled. "Dante was tiny like that when he was born. Now look how big he's grown."

He turned and studied her again. "You really okay or are you pushing things?"

"I really will be fine. Let's find Dante."

Mariella was wearing clothes lent to her by a nurse on the night shift. Her feet didn't bother her much. The cut on the left gave her a bit of a limp, but the doctor had assured her it would heal quickly with no lasting damage. The scruffy slippers she wore needed to be replaced, too. Her mind spun with all she needed to do.

Cristiano led the way into the pediatric ward and in seconds they were in the room with the baby.

"The pediatrician made his round a short time ago," the nurse said. "Your baby's ready to go." She smiled at both of them. "He's a darling child. So attentive. But I know he misses his parents."

In a moment Mariella stood by the crib. Dante looked up at Mariella and gave her a wide grin. Lifting his arms, he came up easily when she reached out to pick him up. She held him closely, relishing the warmth of him in her arms. Her heart swelled with love. For a moment she almost broke into tears thinking about how close she had come to losing him. He was her precious son. The last link to her dearest friend. She gave silent thanks for his safety.

She turned to Cristiano. "You did a wondrous thing saving us. How could I ever thank you?" Mariella took a deep breath, taking in the sweet scent of baby powder and baby shampoo.

"Just get well fast. I'm glad I was there."

"And knew what to do. I don't even want to think about what could have happened."

"Don't. Let's get out of here," he said. "I'm not a big fan of hospitals."

As soon as they stepped outside he steered her to the black sports car parked nearby. Eying it dubiously, she asked, "Do you have a car seat for Dante?"

"The hospital is lending us one until you buy another. Then we'll bring it back. First thing, you need some clothes. Not that the outfit you're wearing doesn't have a certain cachet," he said, opening the door and pushing the passenger seat forward to access the baby's seat.

She laughed, then broke into coughing again. "Thanks. Nothing boosts a woman's ego more than compliments—" She stopped abruptly, before saying *from a man she cares about*. She had only just met the man. Taking the opportunity to end the statement while she put Dante into the carrier, she vowed to watch what she said in future.

Dante was oblivious to any tension. He babbled away in baby language and patted Mariella's face. Tangling his fingers in Mariella's long hair as she leaned over fastening the straps, he pulled.

"Ouch. You have to stop doing that," Mariella said with a laugh, grabbing his little hand and kissing the fingers. "That hurts!"

"He seems in fine form," Cristiano said.

Mariella smiled. "Seems as if no harm done. He's not even coughing."

Once she got Dante situated, she turned to Cristiano, so glad he'd come for her. "I have a million things to do. Are you sure you're up for it?"

"Who else?"

She bit her lip and nodded. Who else indeed? She had

no one except friends in Rome. If he was willing, she'd take all the help she could get.

"I have no identification—it burned in the fire. Along with all my money. I guess the first stop should be the bank, to see if I can get some cash."

"If not, I'll advance you some. Come on, it's breezy, let's get going."

Fifteen minutes later Mariella sat in a branch of her bank, talking with a manger to verify her identity and get money. Dante sat in Cristiano's lap, reaching for things on the manager's desk. He patiently pulled him back each time.

"That takes care of that,' the manager said as he hung up his telephone. "I'll get my secretary to bring you the money, and a temporary check book. You'll get imprinted checks sent to your home."

"Thank you. I appreciate all you've done for me."

The speedy transaction had been facilitated by Cristiano. The manager knew him and his family.

Once Mariella had money, Cristiano drove to a department store where she could get all she needed. He knew his way around Monta Correnti, for which she was grateful.

First purchase was a stroller for Dante, and a baby carrier. Once she no longer had to carry him, she felt better able to cope.

"Get a few things for him. I'll watch him, then, while you get your things," Cristiano suggested.

"You are a saint to do all this for me," she said. "I'm not sure I could have managed on my own."

He reached out and brushed back a lock of hair, tucking it behind her ear. The touch sent shockwaves running through her body. She smiled shyly and wanted to catch his hand and hold onto it, gaining what strength she could from him. But she kept still, treasuring the touch of his fingertips.

"You could have managed, I have no doubt. But why do it on your own?"

She nodded, knowing he'd made a special effort to help her. From comments Signora Bertatali had made, Cristiano had not left Lake Clarissa since he had arrived. She didn't know why he made an exception for her, but she was grateful.

"Next should be food for the baby. Once he's ready to eat, he lets everyone know in no uncertain terms—crying his head off."

"I bow to your assessment."

Mariella enjoyed shopping, the easy banter that grew between them. She held up baby clothes for his approval, which he gave after much mock deliberation.

"It really doesn't matter that much," she said, laughing at his posturing about the perfect outfit for Dante. "He's a baby. He doesn't know or care what he wears."

"Hey, he's special. He needs to make a statement—he's cool and he knows it."

She laughed again. Who could have suspected the devastation of the fire could lead to such a fun day-after? "I'll be sure to take pictures so he'll know when he's older."

Cristiano cocked his head at that. "Do you have a camera?"

"It burned."

"We'll get another."

"All the pictures I had on it are gone, too."

"All the more reason to make sure you start snapping new photos, so those won't be missed."

Her coughing was the only flaw in the day. She bought enough clothes to take care of a few days, shoes that didn't hurt her foot, and cosmetics—a definite necessity when she saw her face in the mirror. She probably should think about returning home to Rome. But she was enjoying every moment with Cristiano. She didn't want to think about being practical just yet.

Cristiano stood outside the dressing room, waiting for Mariella. Dante had been fed, changed, and was now asleep in the stroller. Idly he pushed it back and forth, but the baby didn't need soothing, he was out for his nap.

Glancing around the department store, he noted he was the only man, except for an elderly gentleman talking with his wife. If he'd ever suspected he'd be watching a baby this October day, that would have surprised him. Yet he couldn't imagine letting Mariella and Dante face this alone.

She came out of the dressing room wearing jeans that should have been banned—they made her figure look downright hot. The long-sleeve pink top highlighted her coloring and made her eyes seem even brighter silver. He could look at her all day. It wasn't just her looks that made it easy on the eyes. Her innate optimism shone from her eyes. He wished he could capture some of that for himself.

"Okay, I've gotten all I need, just have to pay for everything," she said, with a bright smile at him and a quick check for Dante.

"I'll be right here," he said, watching with appreciation as she walked away. Those freckles across her nose called to him. He wondered if she liked them. He'd heard from his sister when growing up that most women did not want freckles. He found them enticing. In fact, the more he saw of Mariella, the more he found enticing. She was pretty, sexy, and nurturing. He liked watching her with Dante. The baby seemed as fascinated with her as Cristiano was. "Probably a male thing," he murmured to the sleeping baby.

"All set," she said a moment later.

"Let's eat. You have to be hungry after all this and I know I am."

"Great. Where? Oh, dumb question, you probably always eat at your family restaurant."

Cristiano felt the comment like a slap. He had not been to Rosa for a long time. He'd been avoiding his cosseting family as much as he could, not wanting their sympathy over his injuries, and especially not wanting them to learn of his torment.

Excuses surged to mind. "I thought we'd eat closer to where we are. Rosa is across town. Then we need to get you two back to Lake Clarissa."

"Why? Where am I going to stay?"

"You could stay with me," he said. Then stared at her as the words echoed. Was he totally crazy? He'd been avoiding people to keep quiet about the flashbacks. He could not have anyone stay at the cottage. The first night he had a nightmare, the secret would be revealed.

"Thank you, really, but I can't stay with you. If the Bertatalis have another cabin available, maybe I'll stay a bit longer. I probably ought to return to Rome."

"Don't go."

He felt the intensity of her gaze. He could almost feel her mind working as she considered staying.

"Maybe for a few more days. I have no picture of Ariana to show around, few clothes, no computer."

"I have one you can use."

She slowly smiled. It was all Cristiano could do to refrain from leaning over and kissing her right in the middle of the department store. He caught his breath and forced himself to look away. Had he gone completely round the bend? He'd never felt such a strong desire to kiss a woman before. Obviously complete isolation was driving him more crazy than he already was.

"Then I'll stay for a few more days."

A man in his situation couldn't ask for more than that. At least not yet.


When Cristiano drove into the village by the lake, Mariella felt her stress level rise. The horror of the fire rose the closer they got to the resort. She wondered if she could ever fall asleep without fearing a fire would consume her lodgings.

He stopped the car near the Bertatalis' residence. The charred remains of the cottage could be seen clearly in the daylight. How had the fire started?

Signora Bertatali must have heard them as she threw open her door and rushed out to Mariella.

"Ah, Signorina Holmes. You are back." She hugged Mariella, baby and all. "I am so thankful. And the baby, he is well?" She greeted Cristiano and insisted on all coming into her home.

"We are devastated your cabin burned. Aye, when I think of what could have happened without the swift intervention of Cristiano. You will stay with us at no cost, we insist. That such a thing could happen is not acceptable. The fire chief thinks the heater's wiring overloaded. All are being inspected before we rent out another space. The electrician is here even now. I am so sorry. When I think of what could have happened—"

"We're fine, signora."

Cristiano nodded at her acknowledgment, staying near the door.

"Our insurance will cover everything. Please say you'll stay a little longer. We do not want you to remember Lake Clarissa with the horror from the fire. Do let us make it up to you. My husband has a contractor going over every inch of every cottage. They will be totally safe. I guarantee it. Please stay."

Mariella looked at Cristiano. "A day or two," she agreed.

"I am so grateful you are safe. And your baby. Come, let me prepare some tea and you sit. Please, come into the kitchen."

Signora Bertatali bustled around asking question after question. How did she feel? Did she get enough clothing?

"We are all so fortunate you saw the fire," she said to Cristiano. "How did you from your grandfather's cottage?"

He explained he'd been riding. Mariella wondered why he'd gone riding in the middle of the night. Not that it mattered. Thanks to him, they were safe.

Signora Bertatali poured the hot tea and sat at the table across from Mariella and Cristiano. Dante began fussing and Mariella reached into the baby bag to bring out a bottle. In short order it was ready.

"Let me. You drink your tea," Cristiano said, reaching for the little boy. Dante was light in his arms. For a moment Cristiano saw the baby he'd rescued. How was that child doing all these months later? He would have to see if he could find out.

"Thank you."

"And you, Cristiano, your family will be even more proud to learn of your rescue of last night. After that terrorist attack in Rome. I shiver every time I think about it."

He had no comeback. He didn't care if his family never knew of last night's fire. He was content to know he'd been able to function as his training had prepared him. No fear except for the woman and child.

Once Dante had been fed and changed, Signora took

them to the cottage right next door to the Bertatalis' home. It had been completely checked out and declared safe. Cristiano unpacked his car and brought in all her new clothes while Mariella put the baby down in the new crib.

Too tired to think straight, she thanked him and watched as he left, then fell on top of the bed and pulled over a blanket. Before she could mentally list any of the many steps she needed to take, she fell asleep.

The next morning Cristiano sat on the flagstone patio in front of the cottage and read from the latest manual his commander had sent him. Still technically on disability leave, he had plenty of time to keep up with the latest information and his commander agreed, sending him updates and reports to keep him current.

He heard a sound and looked up, surprised to see Mariella walking down the long graveled driveway. The sun turned her hair a shimmery molten gold shot through with strands of copper. She wore dark trousers and a sweater, though the afternoon was warm for October. He hadn't expected to see her here. How had she found the cottage? Not that it was hidden, lying right off the main road.

*"Buongiorno,"* she called in greeting.

"Hello," he said, rising as he placed the manual face down on the small table. He hadn't expected her to make the long walk up a hill with a cut on her foot. Where was the baby?

"I came to say thank you for saving us," she said.

"You did that yesterday," he said, watching as she walked closer. He could see no lasting effects of the fire. Only the faintest hint of a limp showed.

"I know. I just wanted to see you again." She gave a shy smile and the effect on his senses was like the sun coming out after days of rain. For a moment, he felt elation. Then common sense intruded. He'd asked her to stay in Lake Clarissa, she had. Now she probably wondered why.

He glanced around. It was warm in the sun, but would cool down when the patio became shaded by the trees.

"Would you like something to drink?" he asked. He hadn't had anyone at the cottage since he had arrived. It felt strange to invite her inside.

"A glass of water sounds nice. It's warmer than I thought it would be today and that's a long walk."

"Especially with an injured foot."

She lifted her leg slightly and rotated the foot in question. "Actually, it didn't bother me that much."

He stared at the foot, then let his gaze wander up her body to those freckles. Her hair was curly and framed her pretty face. Her eyes were more silvery now than the other night. Then they'd been a stormy grey. The sun highlighted her hair, some of it the color of honey, some almost white gold. He wanted to touch those silky strands to see if they were as soft as they promised to be. Brush his fingertips across the freckles that dusted her face. Kiss her and feel the rise of desire being with a beautiful woman evoked. Prove to himself he was still alive, healthy and normal.

He resisted temptation. Dared he take the risk?

Every cell in his body clamored for closer contact with her. Temptation was never easily denied. He relished the feelings, the wanting, the anticipation, the desire. After staying alone for months, it was like an awakening, as if his body were coming alive after a long illness, painfully tingling. How ironic, he was attracted to a woman for the first time in ages and he dared not pursue the relationship. At least not beyond a casual friendship.

"Water's in the kitchen," he said.

She tilted her head slightly and smiled. "Usually is."

He led the way through the dark living area back to the kitchen. He opened the cupboard and stared for a moment. There were no glasses.

She followed him, looking around with curiosity. For a moment Cristiano scanned the room, noting the dirty dishes stacked in the sink.

He heard a giggle behind him and turned to find Mariella trying to hide her laughter. He scowled, knowing exactly what she was thinking.

"I've seen college kids with digs like this, but I never thought once people were grown up they'd continue to live this way. Or is it only guys?" she asked, the amusement bubbling in her voice.

"Dante would understand," he said, spotting a glass on the counter. He snagged it and quickly washed it. After it was rinsed, he filled it with tap water and handed it to her, still dripping. His sister would have his head if she ever saw the mess. His father would be speechless. Cristiano remembered how fastidious Luca had always been in the kitchen of Rosa.

She took the glass with a smile. "Thank you. I didn't mean to offend," she said. Drinking the entire glass in less than a minute, she held it out for more.

He filled it again. She coughed until she had tears in her eyes. Taking the glass, she sipped it more slowly this time, her gaze looking around the room as a smile tugged her lips.

"I've been recovering from an injury," he said gruffly, suddenly wanting her to know he didn't normally live this way.

Instant compassion shone in her face when she swung back. "I'm sorry. And on top of that you had the ordeal of carrying me away from the fire. I can't believe how fast the cottage burned."

"Entire houses can burn in less time given the right fuel and no safety precautions," he said. "How's the baby?"

"He's doing well. The Bertatalis are bending over backward to be accommodating. Did you know she has three children of her own, all grown now? She says she loves babies and almost begged to watch Dante for me while I walked here. Her husband has offered to take me on one of the fishing excursions on the lake."

"He leads fishing expeditions in the summer. Take him up on it if you get the chance—you'll like it."

"Hmm, maybe. It seems a little cool to be boating."

"I'll give you a ride back when you're ready to leave. Save walking on that foot."

"That would put you out. Which was not my intention. I truly wanted to thank you. You're a hero."

"No, I'm not." Why did people keep saying that? If they knew the truth— "I'll give you a ride," he said.

His motorcycle sat beneath the carport at the rear. Beyond that was a small building, door firmly closed.

Mariella followed, glancing around the kitchen again as she stepped outside.

"I could come back tomorrow and clean up the kitchen for you. As a token of appreciation."

Cristiano shook his head. "I don't need it."

He started the bike and helped her climb on. Instructing her to hold on tight, he didn't expect the jolt of awareness when she wrapped her arms around him. Her body was pressed against his back, her hands linked over his stomach. He closed his eyes, relishing the feel of her. Her hands were small, gripping over his belly. Her breasts pressed against his back and for a moment he wanted to turn around and pull her into a kiss.

"So how long will Signora Bertatali watch Dante?" he asked.

"No time limit."

"Want to take the long way home?"

"Sure."

"Will you be warm enough?"

"Oh, yes."

He started out slowly and then picked up speed when they reached the road. Turning away from the lake, he took the road he loved to ride when trying to outrun the demons and nightmares. It wound through the forest, dappled in shade in places, in full sunshine in others.

From time to time they could catch a glimpse of the lake sparkling in the distance. It was not as breezy today as other days and in places the lake looked like a mirror, reflecting sky and forest.

Mariella loved the ride. She felt free with the scenery whipping by. Seeing the lake when they turned from time to time was fabulous. Thankful for her rescue, she felt especially attentive to everything today. It was as if she were seeing things in a different light.

All due to Cristiano. And not only because he had saved them from the fire. But to take time yesterday to make sure she and Dante had all they needed was special.

But what she cherished the most was his request for her to stay.

He slowed and pulled off the road in a turn out that went to the edge of the open space in front of them.

"Oh wow," she said, gazing at the sight. The lake looked like a jewel nestled in a green setting. Beyond another hill and then another rose, until she felt she were on the rim of the world, looking out.

He stopped the motor. The silence was complete. Then the soft sighing of the breeze through the trees could be heard.

"This is beautiful," she said softly, so as not to disturb the moment.

"We can walk to the edge if you like," he said.

She hopped off the motorcycle and waited for him. Walking to the edge, she saw several rough-cut log benches.

"Others must come here for the view," she said, sitting on one sun-warmed log.

He sat beside her, gazing at the vista in front of them.

For several moments neither spoke, then Cristiano said softly, "I come here when I need to get away."

"A special place," she said, smiling, feeling as if she'd been given a gift. "I wish I had one. It gets overwhelming sometimes with Dante and working and trying to balance everything. I would love a place like this to just sit and be."

He nodded. "Maybe that's what is appealing, I can just be myself here."

She looked at him, tilting her head slightly. "Can't you be yourself everywhere?"

He met her gaze and slowly shook his head. "People expect certain things."

"And we always try to meet those expectations." She sighed. "Probably why I feel so inadequate with Dante. I expect to be wise like my mother and I'm not."

"She probably wasn't that wise when you were six months old," he said gently.

Mariella thought about that for a while. Was it true? Had her mother been learning as she went? "You might be right, but she always seemed to know what to say, how to explain things."

"You're a good mother to Dante. Don't doubt yourself."

Unexpectedly, Cristiano reached out and took her hand,

resting their linked fingers on his thigh. "It's beautiful here in winter when it looks as if powder sugar has been sprinkled on the trees. Now the trees are changing color, but spring will bring the new green of beginning leaves."

"Thanks for bringing me here," she said, returning her gaze to the magnificent view. The carefree feeling continued as if she had let all her worries vanish on the ride and the reward was this unexpected beauty.

They talked softly until the sun started slipping behind some of the trees and the temperature began to drop.

"Time to go," he said.

Mariella nodded, reluctant to end the enchantment of the afternoon. She would never forget this.

He continued the loop arriving in the village near the resort. He continued to the center of town to drop her by the small grocery store where she said she needed to pick up some things for Dante.

"Thanks for the ride home," she said, when she had dismounted. Giving into impulse, she kissed his cheek. "See you," she said and turned swiftly to enter the store.

Cristiano watched as she walked away, so alive and happy. He didn't want to think of the outcome had he not been riding that night.

But he felt like an impostor. He was no hero. He'd never tell her, or anyone, how fear engulfed him. How the nightmares of that incident in May haunted him unexpectedly day and night. Why couldn't he get the images out of his mind? Granted he could go several days without them. Just when he'd think he had it licked, they'd spring up and threaten to render him powerless.

Though he had been able to cope at the fire. Maybe, maybe, he was getting over it.

Mariella entered the grocery store and glanced back through the glass door. Cristiano sat on his motorcycle, staring at the door. Could he see her? She felt her heart beating heavily. She had never ridden a motorcycle before. She'd not known how intimate it felt, pressed against his hard body, feeling his muscles move against her as he drove the powerful bike. She still felt tingly and so aware of him. She hated to move, but people would begin to wonder if she stayed at the door staring like a moonstruck teenager at her latest heartthrob.

She almost giggled as she forced herself to move.

Would she ever get the chance to ride behind him again? Visit his special spot? Life seemed especially sweet today. It could almost as easily have been over for her. Instead, she had ridden with a sexy guy who intrigued her, fascinated her, set her hormones rocking.

She was curious about the injuries he was recovering from. Maybe he'd re-injured himself rescuing her, though he looked to be in perfect health to her. His broad shoulders and muscles beneath the shirt he'd worn attested to robust health. He looked as if he could jump mountains. And obviously was strong enough to carry her and the baby from a burning building.

With the loss of all her things—especially her computer—the sooner she returned home, the sooner she could pick up the pieces of her life. Maybe it was a sign she was not to look for Dante's father.

Fortunately her purchases fit into two bags and Mariella carried them back to the cottage. She also brought a bouquet of mixed mums for her hostess. She wanted to brighten the woman's day in gratitude for watching Dante for her. She wished the Bertatalis didn't feel so guilty. They had not known of the faulty wiring. All had ended well—except for the loss of her computer.

Was there a place in town she could use one? An Internet

café? Or, she could take Cristiano up on his offer and use his. Well, that was a no-brainer.

The next morning after tidying up, bathing and dressing the baby, Mariella set off for Cristiano's house. The road to the cottage was lightly traveled and easily navigated. However, it proved awkward pushing the baby stroller down the uneven graveled driveway.

The day was a copy of yesterday, sunny and balmy. Leaves had begun to change on some of the trees covering the hillside, bright spots of yellows and reds showed brilliant in the sunshine against the deep green of the conifers. She breathed the fresh air. What would it be like to live here year round? Nothing like New York where she'd been the past four years, with its concrete canyons and few open parks beyond Central Park.

Different from Rome, too. But that was home. Crowded, frenetic, yet comfortably providing all she really needed.

Rounding the bend, she saw the cottage. She studied it as she walked toward it. It was warm cream-colored stone, with a steep pitched roof of dark slate. The windows were wide with shutters on either side. It looked old, settled, perfect for its mountain backdrop. With an ageless look, it was hard to tell when it was built, but clearly a long time ago, she suspected from what she'd seen on the inside. He was lucky to have such a comfortable place to recuperate.

Cristiano was not on the patio this morning. She walked to the front door and knocked.

Cristiano opened the door a moment later and stared at her in surprise, then at the baby, his expression softening.

"What are you two doing here?" he asked, smiling at Dante.

"I came to take you up on your offer to use your computer. I need to check in with my clients."

"Come on in." He opened the door wide and she pushed the carriage in.

"It's dark in here," Mariella said, stepping into the living room. "Why is it all closed up?"

He looked around as if seeing the heavy drapes pulled over the windows for the first time.

"It suited me."

"How odd."

"They help insulate the windows."

"It's not that cold."

He stared at her a moment, then shrugged. "I'll get the laptop."

In less than five minutes, Dante was happily kicking his legs from the baby seat playing with a spoon and plastic cup while Mariella booted up the computer on the kitchen table. Cristiano had hooked it to a phone line. It wouldn't be the fastest connection, but at least she could check her email. Once Cristiano saw she was connected, he took off to give her privacy. She appreciated that, too aware of the man to concentrate on her work if he hovered nearby.

She gazed around the room while the computer booted up. It had a certain old-world charm that she loved. There was a huge fireplace, stone-cold now, at one end. She could envision a cheerful fire in the dead of winter when a sprinkle of snow might lie on the ground. How cozy this room would be. The large wooden table would seat a family of eight. The stone floor was cold, but, with a few rugs, could be comfortable in the winter months.

Which she would never see here in Lake Clarissa. For a moment the disappointment seemed too strong to bear.

# CHAPTER FOUR

DANTE became fussy. Mariella prepared a mid-morning bottle and picked up the baby. She did not want to sit in one of the wooden chairs by the large table, balancing the baby and bottle, so she wandered into the living room. She'd like to tidy this room or at least open the curtains so she could see the magnificent views.

Sitting in a wing chair, she fed Dante, softly crooning to him as he ate. Maybe the dimness worked to her advantage as Dante began to fall asleep just as he finished the bottle.

Mariella continued to hold him after he fell asleep, relishing this quiet time with just the two of them. He was a beautiful child with dark brown eyes and dark hair. Ariana would have so loved this child of hers. Would Dante resemble her when he grew older? Or his unknown father? Tears threatened every time Mariella remembered her friend and her untimely death. How could she have borne having to leave this child behind? Love expanded within her heart and she wanted to hold the moment forever.

Cristiano came into the room from outside.

"Snack time?" he asked, studying her and Dante. He sat in the chair near her.

"Mid-morning feed." She gazed down at her sleeping baby. "I'll put him in the stroller and go when he wakes up. I still have to follow up on some work I was doing. I appreciate your letting me use your computer. We'll stay out of your way."

She rose and carefully placed the baby in the carrier, covering him lightly with a soft blanket.

"You're not in the way. Finish your work, then stay for lunch."

Cristiano knew he was grasping at straws, but he wanted her to stay. He wanted to talk to her, watch her laugh. Her skin was flushed slightly and looked soft and warm. Her hair curled around her cheeks, down her back. The sweater showed off the feminine body that awakened a need in his he'd thought long gone. When she was nearby, he had to fight the urge to find out more about her, see what she liked and didn't like.

And fight not to kiss her.

When he realized his thoughts had stayed on that point, he quickly looked away.

"You know that fire scared me. What if something happens to me? Who will take care of Dante?" she asked, covering the baby with a light blanket.

Cristiano's mother had died when he was a small boy. He remembered her smile, the fragrance she wore. The almost tangible love she'd given. No one got fully used to losing a parent. Had his father felt the same as Mariella? Worried about his children should something happen to him? Yet it wasn't the same. His father's sister lived in Monta Correnti, for most of his childhood Cristiano's grandfather had lived in this cottage with the rest of the family. There had always been family around. But one never got over the loss of his mother.

"My mother's dead, too," he said slowly.

"But not your father?"

"No, he's doing well." He guessed he was. Surely some-one would have told him if he weren't. Not that he'd been very receptive to overtures from his family since he'd taken up residency in the cottage. His bossy sister had made sure he knew her thoughts on that from the messages she left.

The flashbacks happened without warning. He couldn't be around people who knew him for long—they'd see how messed up he was and cosset him so much he'd never get his life back. He had to beat this thing.

Mariella gazed at him as if expecting him to say more. He stared at her for a moment, wondering if he was finally moving on. He had handled the cottage fire. He had not had a nightmare since that night. He drew a breath, smell-ing the sweet scent of Mariella. It brought a yearning that grew in strength every time he was with her. Yet he could not fall for this woman.

"Are you the oldest child?"

"Yes, Isabella is a close second, incredibly bossy. Our mother died when I was a child. She took on the house-hold work, and tried to keep us in line." For a moment he remembered some of the happy days they'd spent at the cottage, playing at the lake, just being with family. Life had thrown curves he'd never expected when he had been a child.

"Do your brother and sister still live close by?"

"Isabella still lives in Monta Correnti, along with Valentino," he said, smiling at the thought of his family.

"So you get to see them a lot. Must be nice. I was an only child."

He didn't reply. He had not seen them since they had visited him in the hospital after the bombing. His hospital stay had been lengthy and he'd missed his brother's wed-ding, and his cousin Lizzie's. Since his release from hospital Isabella called every so often trying to get him to go to family events. Mostly he let the answering machine take her call.

A lot had happened in his family over the recent months, including the startling revelation that his father had two older children by a first marriage. Cristiano still wasn't sure what to think about that. He had not met the two men—twins who had been raised in America. It was odd to think they shared the same father.

So far he'd found excuses that didn't raise undue suspicions. He was running out of time, however. How long could he keep his problem from his family? He wanted it to go away, wanted life back the way it had been.

He had loved this place as a child. It had been the first spot he'd thought of when wanting to retreat. His family was busy, fortunately. No one spent much time here anymore. Hiding hadn't changed a thing. Maybe he should open curtains. He was not in a tight subway tunnel, but had a view of endless miles.

"This is a terrific room. Do you use the fireplace when it gets cold?" she asked as she headed for the kitchen.

"Of course. It's the primary source of heat," he said, nodding toward the large wood-burning fireplace along an outside wall. He remembered rainy days in the fall when he and his brother Valentino would spend hours in front of the fire, trucks and cars zooming around. He hadn't seen his brother in months; he realized suddenly how much he missed him.

Cristiano followed her into the kitchen. She sat at the table and began checking her account. He crossed to the sink and leaned on the edge of the counter looking out the window over it. The view out back was opposite to the lake, to the rolling tree-covered hills that rose so high, offering peace and serenity. Dots of color presaged the coming of winter. Five months ago he had been working in Rome, settled with his life, his friends. Now he was practically a hermit, his closest friend dead, his job on hold.

But the hills didn't care. They remained the same year in and year out. Steadfast, secure, unchanging. It gave a longer perspective than short-time occurrence. Would he recover fully? Or was it time to begin to think of another way to earn a living? Would he return to Rome and the life he'd so enjoyed, or remain a virtual recluse cut off from friends and family?

"That was easy," she said a few moments later.

He looked over.

"Hardly any mail. I did send a note to two clients telling them I might be another day or two getting back in touch. Tomorrow I'll see about getting another laptop. Maybe in a shop in Monta Correnti."

"You are dedicated. I thought you were on vacation."

She looked at him. "I am, but I don't consider myself any more dedicated than you going into a burning building to save lives when you're recovering from injuries. You know I'll be forever grateful. Keep that in your heart. Now, do you have a printer?"

"Not here, why?"

"I wanted to print out a picture of Ariana. I found one I could use. The one I brought with me burned in the fire."

"Sorry. There's an Internet café in Monta Correnti, near the church on the plaza. They'd have a printer."

She shut down the computer and closed the top. "I'll go there, then. Thanks for the use of your computer today." She leaned back in the chair and looked at him. "So tell me, how did you get into firefighting? I think that's one of the most dangerous lines of work anywhere—pitting your life against a raging fire," she said.

"I like making a difference." A ready answer. It didn't explore the variety of reasons he chose fighting fires as compared to police work or mountain rescue. But all were similar kinds of jobs—first responders, never knowing what would await them. Challenges to be surmounted. Never boring.

She smiled, her eyes sparkling silver. Her hair shone in the sunshine pouring in through the side window.

Cristiano had a stronger urge to reach out and twirl some of those tresses around his fingers, feeling the silky softness, the heat from each warm strand. Those desires rose each time he saw her.

"Did your father want you to do something else?" she asked.

"Probably, though he never pressured any of us. My sister works with him at the family restaurant. My brother Valentino is home less than I am."

"Is your brother Valentino Casali? The racing daredevil?" She looked surprised.

Cristiano nodded. He knew Valentino had a reputation to match his daredevil ways. For the first time he wondered if their decisions had hurt their father. He took such pride in Rosa. It was a fine restaurant, but only Isabella had followed their father's path and worked in the family establishment.

"He got married recently, I saw that somewhere," she said. "Not my idea of a married man."

Cristiano shrugged. "What would be your idea of a married man?"

"Someone faithful."

"Valentino is fiercely loyal. He would always be faithful," Cristiano was quick to say.

"I'd also want my husband home more than he seems to be. And safe."

"Maybe now that he has a home and wife, he'll change. People do, you know."

She nodded.

"Other attributes?"

She frowned in thought for a moment. "Fun to be with, able to talk and share, and I'd want a husband to want the same things I do."

"Sounds like you've thought about it for a while."

"Ariana and I used to talk about our dream man. Hers turned out not to be the dream."

"And you?"

"Haven't met him yet. So what do you do here all day? Not working. No television I saw," she asked.

"This and that." He should tell her about the woodworking. Maybe later he'd take her to the shed to see.

"Did you always want to be a virtual assistant?" he asked, finding it an odd sort of job for such a bubbling personality like hers. He'd picture her surrounded by office workers, working as a team player, not in a solo job from home.

"When in university in New York, I planned to hit Madison Avenue big time. I majored in marketing—American style. But then my parents died, then Ariana. Things changed so much, I couldn't manage that on top of watching Dante. Maybe someday."

"I think I heard the baby," he said, hearing a noise in the living room.

Mariella jumped to her feet and went to check on Dante. Two minutes later she came back, carrying a bubbling baby.

"He was kicking his feet and saying something. I can't wait for him to talk."

"I'll start our lunch. I'll make you some of the world's best marinara sauce."

"The world's best?" she scoffed lightly.

"Hey, I challenge you to find better. It's from the family's restaurant. And you'll thank your lucky stars you get to have some."

"You made it?"

"No. My sister sends me care packages. I freeze the sauce until I'm ready to use it. It won't take long to prepare."

"Time enough for me to feed this little guy, then," she said.

"Again?"

"He eats a lot, that's why he's growing."

Cristiano took the sauce from the freezer, peeled off the wrapper and dropped it into a pan. Soon it began to simmer on the stove as he boiled water for pasta. He watched Mariella feed Dante while he worked. For the first time in months, he felt a touch of optimism. There was something about cooking long-familiar foods and sharing that touched that part of him that had once liked to spend time with friends. Stephano had loved the marinara sauce and every time he learned Isabella had sent some, he'd invite himself and his family over for dinner. He and the other guys at the station urged him to bring in enough for everyone.

For once the memory of his friend and the time they'd shared didn't hurt with the searing pain of loss. It was a bittersweet memory of times that would never come again. He missed his friend and probably always would.

But life went on. Stephano had loved life so much, he would have personally come to Lake Clarissa and knocked some sense into his head if he'd known Cristiano was secluding himself like this.

Except—the flashbacks were real.

Mariella's laugh pulled him from his thoughts and he looked up. The baby had something smeared all over his face, and his pudgy hands were spreading the mess to his hair.

"What is that?"

"Some kind of oatmeal cereal. The pediatrician is having me try it. Probably tastes like paste and feels better spread around outside than eating," she said, trying to catch Dante's hands to wipe them. She giggled. "He's a mess. I'm thinking this is not one of the better ideas the doctor had."

"You think? Hey, little man, would you like some of my papa's sauce?"

"He's not even six months yet. Too young for big people food."

"A taste won't hurt." Cristiano dipped his pinkie into the warming sauce and then carried it to the baby. Dante grabbed his hand and pulled it to his mouth. His frown of surprise had them both laughing.

"Maybe it's an acquired taste," Cristiano said.

The baby had eaten and Mariella settled him on a thick blanket on the floor when Cristiano served up their lunch.

"Wow, this was definitely worth waiting for," Mariella said after her first bite. "What makes it so great?"

"Family secret," he said.

"Ah. I bet Rosa has a line waiting for tables every night."

"The economy these days makes things unsettled. It does well enough, I think." Actually, from one or two comments Isabella had made, Cristiano wondered if that was true. Maybe he should check into it. If there was a problem, he might be able to help financially; he had some money saved.

"I know people are cutting back, but good food is always relished."

"My sister has been pestering me to talk about the situation for a while. It's her area, not mine. Whatever she decides is fine with me."

"Um. I just hope she decides to keep making this wonderful sauce. Does she sell it by the jar?"

He shook his head.

"She should. Maybe I can talk to her about that. She could consider an Internet mail-order business on the side. I bet folks would pay a premium. It obviously freezes well. I wonder how it could be shipped?"

"Ever the marketer?"

She nodded, but continued to look thoughtful.

"You said you went to university in New York? What was that like? Why there?"

"My dad was American, but he settled in Rome ages ago. Ever since I can remember the plan was for me to attend school there when I hit university level. After their death, it helped that New York is vastly different from Rome, so I didn't have lots of memories to deal with at every turn. Maybe it helped with the grief, too. To have the coursework to concentrate on."

"So now you're back settled in Rome?" he asked.

"I'm Italian, so is Dante. There is nothing waiting for us in New York. When he's older, I'll take him there and show him the sights. It's a fantastic city. But it's not home."

She looked up. "It was good to grow up in Rome, but I'm wondering if it might be even better to have a smaller town, where I could build a support group. A single mom will need help. I've lost touch with many of my friends from high school."

And lost her best friend, he remembered.

"I couldn't wait to move to Rome when I graduated. More vibrant, more things to do."

"Of course. But when you got hurt, you came home. There's a lot to be said for a country setting. Where in Rome can you get views like you have? Sitting on the patio, seeing the lake, the gorgeous hills. It's fantastic."

"Doesn't offer a lot of opportunity for young people, though."

"Ah, but that depends on what opportunities one's looking for. I have a job, a child. My opportunities now lie in different areas than when I was single and fancy free."

She smiled again and Cristiano was struck by her happy outlook. She seemed not to have a care in the world, though he knew differently. What was her secret to that optimistic outlook?

Not having to deal with post-traumatic stress disorder, for one thing.

"I think I'll take the baby to the lake later. Want to come with us?" she asked.

"Will it be warm enough for him?" he asked.

"In the sunshine. I guess you've done it a thousand times."

"It never gets old. The lake is beautiful all times of the year. My ankle was broken a while ago. I'm still getting it back in shape. The sooner I'm fit, the sooner I can return to work. Want to go Jet Skiing?"

She laughed and shook her head. "Sitting on the beach is enough."

# CHAPTER FIVE

CRISTIANO drove them in the car back to the village. He and Mariella took the baby to the shore near the marina. The beach was a mixture of sand and pebbles sloping gently to the water's edge. There was a couple sitting in nearby chairs, reading. She waved to them while Cristiano settled on a spot some distance away so as not to disturb their tranquility with their presence.

He brought a blanket and soon Dante was taking tummy time facing away from the water, so he was facing up hill. When he grew frustrated, Mariella sat him up, holding him lightly so he wouldn't fall over. He could almost balance by himself. He settled in first gnawing on the plastic keys, then throwing them down. She retrieved them and handed them back.

Again

And again.

Cristiano stretched out beside them, laughing at the baby's antics. Mariella tossed him the keys.

"You try it," she said.

Dante turned to see the keys and grinned at Cristiano.

"Don't want to lose your keys," he said, dangling them in front of the baby. "Especially when you're older and that means wheels."

The tranquility of the setting soothed. Mariella coughed

again, wishing she'd get over the smoke problem soon. Her chest felt dry and tight. Taking a deep breath, she relished the clean air scented with evergreen. The sun sparkled on the water. In the distance she could see a boat bobbing near the center of the lake. Was that a fisherman?

Dante threw the keys again.

Cristiano retrieved them and handed them to Dante. He threw them again and looked at him, a wide smile on his face. Her heart contracted. She loved this precious baby.

"It's so lovely here, even if we can't swim today. Maybe we'll come back for a visit when Dante's older. Maybe continue the search for his father if we don't find him this time."

"How can you have spent so much time with your friend and not found out more information?"

"She was in the late stages of pregnancy and very ill. We spent more time talking about our shared memories, reliving good times. She changed the subject anytime I brought up who Dante's father might be. He could be named for the man, for all I know. She spoke of what she hoped for in Dante's future. The future she'd never see."

"Maybe she truly didn't want her son to know his father."

"Maybe." She wondered if she was doing wrong trying to find the man. He obviously wasn't as nice as Cristiano. She couldn't imagine any woman not want a child of his to know him.

"It's nice here," she said, turning slightly and fussing with the baby to cover the fact she was studying Cristiano's profile. He made her heart happy. He could have been in movies, she thought. The rugged hero rescuing the heroine from danger then kissing her silly. And her heart almost melted when he played with a baby. Why was a strong man giving his attention to a baby so sexy?

She sighed a bit, wishing he'd pay that much attention to her.

"Problem?" he asked, glancing at her, one eyebrow raised.

"No, just thinking how nice it is here and how horrible the other night was.' She shivered involuntarily. "We could have died."

"But you didn't." His voice came sharp.

She brushed her fingertips over Dante's head. He was perfectly content sitting on the blanket and throwing his plastic keys. She wished she could be so easily satisfied.

"I know that. As a firefighter, you've probably seen lots of death."

He frowned and sat up, resting an arm on his upraised knee. "It's not something anyone gets used to," he said.

"I imagine not." She could have bitten her tongue and not said anything. How many other lives had he saved, and how many had he not been able to save? There was more to firefighting than just pouring water on a fire.

"Do you think I can raise him?" she asked a few moments later.

"You can do anything if you want it enough. Remember that. From what I see, you are doing a fine job."

"Tell me more about growing up around here."

"Weekends are busy times for restaurants. My father worked hard. My mother with him, until she died. But even though we didn't see much of them our childhood was still magical. Especially when my grandfather was alive. His life was different from our everyday life. He knew the trees, the forest, fish in the lake."

She fell silent, thinking about the vacations she and her parents had enjoyed. It seemed so long ago and far away. Would visiting some of the spots bring the memories closer?

Or only emphasize she was alone? She wanted Dante to see all of Italy. They'd make new memories.

"I'm going into Monta Correnti tomorrow. The doctors at the hospital wanted to check me and Dante again, make sure there are no lasting effects. I need to get access to a printer so I can print up another picture of Ariana. Maybe check around in Monta Correnti to see if anyone recognizes her."

"Park near the town square. Easy to get to an Internet café, shops and the hospital."

"We'll find it," she said cheerfully, wishing he'd offered to drive them into town.

After visiting the hospital the next morning and getting a clean bill of health for both her and Dante, Mariella wandered the center part of Monta Correnti. First stop after the hospital was the Internet café where she was able to print a color photograph of Ariana. Staring at the picture of her friend, she remembered how vital she'd always been when younger. The illness had robbed her of so much.

Then she pushed the baby in the stroller, wandering down side streets, walking around the square. When she saw a likely tourist spot, she showed the photo. No one recognized Ariana.

It was after one when Mariella turned back onto the wide piazza and gazed at the buildings. Rosa seemed to leap out at her. That was Cristiano's family's restaurant—the one with the excellent marinara sauce. She pushed the stroller along, wondering if she dared try Dante in the restaurant. So far the baby had been in perfect harmony with all they'd done. But she'd hate to be in the middle of a meal and have him start screaming his head off.

As they approached, Mariella saw a nice open-air space

connected to the restaurant. Much better for the baby, she thought. The day was warm enough to sit outside.

Once seated, with a baby highchair for Dante, Mariella perused the menu. She'd try the tortellini with the famous sauce. She sat back to enjoy the ambiance while waiting for her order. The waiter had brought bread sticks and she gave one to Dante to drool on. He beat the table, put it in his mouth and looked surprised. She laughed. Hadn't he expected it to be food? He couldn't eat it, but she thought he could gum it a bit. Once it got soggy, she replaced it with another.

The courtyard was delightful. Tables were scattered around as if awaiting company, two others occupied. None too close to impede a private conversation. The bougainvillea spilled down a trellis, their flowers faded now as winter approached. She bet they were spectacular in the height of summer. A fountain's melody gave a pleasant sound to soothe and enhance enjoyment of the food. Mariella suspected the restaurant was a favorite of many.

When the meal was placed before her, Mariella smiled in anticipation. She looked at the waiter. "I can't wait to eat this. I had this sauce recently at Cristiano Casali's place. Do you know him?"

The waiter bowed slightly. "Of course. He is son of the owner, Luca." He frowned. "He has not been to visit recently. I shall tell his sister you are here."

Mariella took a bite of the tortellini. It almost melted in her mouth. The sauce was even better than she'd had at Cristiano's. She savored each mouthful.

"Signora?"

A pretty woman wearing an apron approached Mariella.

"*Sì?*"

"I am Isabella, Cristiano's sister. You are a friend of Cristiano?"

Mariella smiled. "He rescued me and my baby from a fire at Lake Clarissa. I consider him a hero."

"Ah. May I?" Isabella said, holding onto the back of a chair.

"Please."

"How is he?" she asked when she sat down.

"Fine. He said he is recovering from injuries?" How odd his sister asked a stranger for an update on her brother.

"He was a first responder to the bombing in Rome last May," Isabella said slowly.

"I knew that. That's where he was injured."

"A burn, a broken ankle. Yet it's taking a long time to heal. Does he walk okay?"

"Fine."

Isabella stared at Mariella for a long moment.

Growing uncomfortable, Mariella smiled again. "I had some of your marinara sauce at Cristiano's and so when I had to come to Monta Correnti and saw the restaurant, I thought I'd eat it again. It's delicious."

"Thank you. So you ate at Cristiano's home?"

"The cottage near the lake," Mariella clarified.

"I know where he's staying. Did he bring you here?" Isabella glanced around quickly.

"No, I drove," Mariella said.

Isabella looked at Dante. "What a blessing he is safe. Cristiano rescued him?"

"We're staying at the cottages rented by the Bertatalis. The unit we rented burned. Faulty wire in the heating device. I was asleep, so was the baby. We both would have been killed if Cristiano hadn't discovered the fire and come in to rescue us."

Isabella smiled. "So like my brother. You are going back to Lake Clarissa today?"

"Yes, for a few more days. I'm on a short holiday." She reached for her bag and pulled out Ariana's picture. "Have you ever seen her?" she asked.

Isabella looked at the photo and handed it back. "No. A friend?"

Mariella nodded. Another story too much to go into with everyone she saw.

"I have something for Cristiano. Would you take it to him for me? Things are hectic right now or I'd go myself. Not that he'd be happy to see me," Isabella said.

"Why ever not?"

"He's been avoiding me. Granted, I've had a few other things on my mind, but I wanted to make sure he was all right. He doesn't answer his phone most of the time. He was conveniently gone from the cottage the two times I went to visit. He's turning into a hermit."

Mariella laughed. "I don't think so. But he can be a bit moody."

"Cristiano? Doesn't sound like him. He has a very even disposition."

"Men hate to be sick. I know my father was grouchy when he was ill. My mother said not to worry, once he was better he'd be back to normal. Maybe Cristiano is frustrated with how long it's taking him to heal and is taking it out on family."

Isabella nodded. "Perhaps, but enough is enough. I shall get the letter and some more sauce. I'm glad to know he's eating what I left, anyway."

"It freezes well. I thought you might consider a mail-order side to the business. I'd love to be able to order this from my home and know I can have it whenever I wish."

"We are just a local restaurant."

"Think about it. I have a degree in marketing and could help set it up if you ever wanted to expand."

Isabella looked at her. "Would it cost a lot?"

"My contribution would be free. I owe Cristiano forever." She reached out and brushed back Dante's hair, smiling at the precious little boy. He rewarded her with a wide smile and drool on his chin mixed with breadcrumbs.

Isabella nodded. "If you would take the letter and sauce to my brother, it will be enough. Tell him his sister asks after him and to call me!"

By the time Mariella was ready to leave, a small bag containing a jar of sauce and an official letter was delivered to her table by the waiter. She placed in it the carry space of the stroller. After wiping Dante's face and hands, she placed him in the stroller and paid her bill. A few moments later they were walking around the square. She studied the restaurant that shared the small piazza with the family restaurant. It looked very upscale and trendy. Not the sort of place for a baby or a casually dressed tourist. Glad she'd had an excellent meal, and that Dante had not raised a fuss, she continued on her walk. There was more to see before returning to the lake.

The town was lovely, decidedly bigger than Lake Clarissa, yet nothing like New York or Rome.

But which appealed to her more these days—the big city excitement or the slower pace in these mountain towns? Would she like to raise Dante in a pastoral setting allowing him to experience nature in its raw beauty? Or would the experiences of museums, art galleries and opera be better to round his education?

Dante had fallen asleep by the time they returned to the car. Mariella couldn't wait to get him home and take a nap herself. The prognosis from the doctor had been good. But she still coughed from time to time.

\* \* \*

The next morning, Mariella put Dante in the stroller, retrieved the sauce Isabella Casali had sent from the refrigerator and headed back up the road to deliver to Cristiano. Her nerves thrummed with anticipation.

On impulse, she stopped at the open-air market and bought a bouquet of mums. The fall flowers were vibrant bronze yellow and purple and she knew they would brighten the kitchen. She hoped he'd appreciate the gesture with the flowers. She wanted to brighten his day as he brightened hers.

Cristiano was sitting on the terrace when she arrived. She smiled when she saw him, already anticipating their time together. There was something about Cristiano that drew her like a lodestone. She watched his expression as it changed from surprise, to pleasure, to cautiousness. He rose and came to meet her.

"*Buongiorno*. We have brought you gifts," she said as she reached the terrace.

"I need no gifts." He watched her from wary eyes. He was several inches taller than she was and she had to crane her neck he was so close.

"Well, the flowers are from Dante, so speak to him about those. And this sack is from your sister, Isabella. She hopes you are well and you should call her."

"My sister?"

"Yes. She says you are becoming a hermit. I told her you weren't. Look how often we visit."

The amusement in his eyes lit a spark in her own.

Her spirits rose. She held out the flowers.

He stared at them and slowly took them. "Dante picked them out?" he asked.

"Well, that was the bunch he made a grab for. I figured they were the ones he wanted to give you."

"Or eat."

She laughed.

Cristiano stole another look at her. She was beautiful when she laughed. It was as if the sun shone from inside, lighting her eyes and making them look like polished silver. That pesky urge to wrap his hands in her hair and pull her closer sprang up again. He looked away before he did something stupid—like give into that impulse.

"And your sister sent you some more sauce." Mariella pulled a brown bag from the back of the stroller and held it out. Cristiano took it. Now both hands were full.

"I'll open the door so you can put the flowers in water and the sauce in the freezer or wherever you wanted to put it. I kept it cold. Delicious, even better made fresh. Still, I think your family could ship it frozen within the country at least. I think the sauce would do quite well—maybe they could send pasta, too. I printed a picture of Ariana, but no one I showed it to yesterday recognized her."

"Did you even take a breath in all that?" he commented, following her into the house and back to the kitchen. He put the sack on the counter, laid the flowers down and rummaged for something to put them in. Finally he settled on a tall glass. The flowers did look nice. But he wasn't used to getting gifts from women and wasn't sure how to handle this.

"I thought they'd look good on the table," she said.

"Sure." He set the flowers on the old table, struck by a memory of his mother doing the same thing. Now the forgotten memory flashed into his mind.

"My mother liked flowers," he said slowly.

"Most people do. I think they look happy. When we stopped at Rosa for lunch after our checkup yesterday, I told the waiter I'd had the sauce before and he apparently told your sister. She came out to meet me."

For a moment Cristiano wished he had given them a

ride, though he wasn't sure about visiting Rosa just yet. He realized he longed to see his father and sister. Find out how things were going at the restaurant. He had to make sure he was all right before risking it. "The outcome from the doctor?"

"We're both healthy. Though I still cough from time to time. The doctor said that would fade. So we had most of the day free after seeing him, so we set out to explore Monta Correnti. I recognized the restaurant as soon as I saw the sign. The food was superb. That's where I met Isabella. There's a letter in the sack for you as well."

Cristiano looked in the sack and took out the envelope. It was from the minister of the interior. Cristiano stared at it. It was addressed to his apartment in Rome and had been forwarded to the restaurant.

"Is it bad news?" Mariella asked, watching him.

"I have no idea." Although deep down Cristiano knew what this letter contained, but did not want to accept it.

"So open it and find out what it says."

He did. The letter confirmed what Cristiano had already known for a long time. He was being awarded a medal of valor for his rescue of the injured from the bombing. Immediately, he crushed the letter and threw it on the counter.

"Um, bad news," she guessed.

He shook his head. "It's a mistake, that's all."

Cristiano didn't want the medal, never had. Why him? Stephano had died. Others from his station had helped with the rescue. There had been so many who died. They had not been able to rescue everyone. Why would anyone want to award him a medal of valor? Especially if they knew of the flashbacks and attacks of sheer terror that gripped him. What kind of man deserved a medal when he couldn't handle all life threw his way?

"What's a mistake?" she asked.

"Never mind. Are you staying?"

"Gee, after such a kind invitation to visit and give you my impressions of Monta Correnti how can I refuse?"

She grinned that cheeky grin and Cristiano almost groaned at the sight. He wanted to pull her into his arms and kiss her until he forgot all the pain of the past. He wanted to feel that slim body against his, driving out the memories and offering an optimistic hope of the future. He wanted to lose himself in her and find that shining optimism she displayed.

He flat out wanted her.

Yet he had deliberately come to Lake Clarissa to avoid people until he could be sure the flashbacks had gone. Wasn't it risky to spend so much time with her? Yet she made him feel normal again, complete. And the baby was adorable. Cristiano wished he could remember when he was so young and innocent the future looked nothing but bright.

Dante began fussing and Mariella shrugged out of her sweater, tossing it on the counter, knocking off the letter. She picked it up and smoothed it out, her eyes drawn to the fancy letterhead. Skimming quickly, she widened them in shock.

"You're getting a medal! How cool is this!"

"I told you, it's a mistake. I don't deserve a medal. I certainly am not a hero!"

Mariella wasn't listening to him. Or attending to Dante, who looked as if he were working up to a fully-fledged screaming bout. She was reading every word in the letter.

"You saved seven people."

"Others saved lives as well."

"And at great personal risk you continued on with the last

two even though you were severely injured," she continued as if she hadn't heard him.

He didn't need the reminder. He saw it over and over every time he had a flashback. The shock, the anguish, the horror.

She looked at him, her eyes shining. "I knew you were a hero. Now it's been confirmed, and not just because of me and Dante. Wow, you must be so proud."

"I'm not going to accept it. It would be a farce."

"But—"

He snatched the paper from her hand, balled it up and tossed it into the trash before storming out of the kitchen.

# CHAPTER SIX

MARIELLA was stunned at his reaction. But she had to see to the fussy baby before going after Cristiano. She lifted the baby from the stroller and tried to soothe him. Preparing a bottle one-handed, she soon shifted him to lie in her arm while offering the bottle. He fussed and pushed it away, wailing as if his world had ended. She jiggled him a little, singing softly as she tried the bottle again. Finally he took it, chewing on the nipple as much as sucking.

"Are you teething, sweetie?" She knew from the baby books that children began teething any time around five or six months, but this was the first time he'd pushed the bottle away. Maybe his gums hurt.

Finally Dante settled down to drink the bottle. Mariella walked into the living room, humming softly as he drank. The curtains were wide open today and sunshine flooded the room. It welcomed her and the baby. She sat in the chair that gave the best view of the lake and continued to hum as she fed Dante.

Her firefighter was an intriguing man. He was a hero, even the ministry confirmed that. Yet he seemed angry about it. Not at all satisfied with the heroic actions he'd performed.

So did that add to the fascination she felt around him? He was drop-dead gorgeous with his thick dark hair and haunted eyes. He looked fit enough to put out a blaze single-handed. She remembered those arms so strong when he lifted her and yet gentle enough for a small baby.

Her heart skipped a beat as she pictured the few times he'd smiled. She could watch him forever, she thought.

Except, he didn't seem to feel the same fascination with her.

Sighing softly, she tried to picture him as a child running around the piazza in Monta Correnti or the restaurant his father owned. She couldn't imagine it. She could see him here at Lake Clarissa, hiking in the woods, swimming in the lake in summer, racing Jet Skis. Chopping wood for a winter's fire. Chasing around a brother who looked like him.

Glancing around the room, she noted how family friendly it was. But she didn't see anything that looked as if it belonged to Cristiano alone. What were his interests? What did he do to combat the stress of rescuing people and battling blazes that threatened life at every turn?

Dante drifted to sleep. She rose and went to the door. As suspected, Cristiano was sitting on the patio, staring at the lake. She would always be able to picture him that way.

"Could you help me?" she asked softly.

He looked around.

"If you would release the back of the stroller, it lies down and I could put the baby there. He'll sleep fine in the stroller and be ready to go when I am."

The man nodded and rose. She watched him, no limp she could see, so why was he still on leave? Was he upset at taking so long to heal after being injured? Champing at the bit, so to speak, to get back to work?

She wondered why he was so adamant against the medal. Sure, others had died, but maybe they were also receiving a medal posthumously.

The stroller was still in the kitchen. He figured out how to recline the back and pulled the half canopy over it. He pushed the stroller, looking just a bit like a giant next to the tiny conveyance, over to Mariella.

She was swaying gently as she held the sleeping baby.

"Thanks, he's getting heavy."

He locked the wheels while she placed the sleeping baby down and covered him with a soft blanket.

"You take to being a mother," he commented, watching her. "Some women don't."

"It's still a struggle." She straightened and looked at the sleeping child with such an expression of love Cristiano caught his breath.

A strand of hair fell across her cheek. Before he could have second thoughts, Cristiano brushed it back, feeling the soft warmth of her skin. He tucked it behind her ear as she looked up and into his eyes. Her smile was warm. Her lips enticing. As if in a dream, he leaned across the slight distance and touched his mouth to hers. She was warm and sweet and so tempting. Kissing her lit a fire in his blood and he wanted the moment to go on forever.

Reality struck when she pulled back and blinked as she looked at him.

"I've wanted to do that for days," he said softly, his hands cupping her cheeks.

"I thought it was only me—I mean that the attraction was just one way."

"Oh, no," he said before he kissed her again, drawing her into his arms, holding her closely while the world seemed to spin around. Mariella was the only thing grounding him.

Rational thought vied with roiling emotions. The desire that rose whenever she was near had to be controlled. He refused to fall for Mariella. She was sweet and young and had bright expectations. He would never falsely lead her on when he had no clue if he could make it in the world again or not.

Holding her, touching her, kissing her, he could forget the horror of that day, the pain of losing his best friend, of the others in the squad that he'd been so close to. But it wasn't fair to her.

Slowly he eased up. They were both breathing hard. He wished for an instant the baby would sleep all afternoon so that he could whisk her into his bedroom and make love until they were both satiated.

"Wow," she said softly, the tip of her tongue skimming her lips. He almost groaned in reaction.

"Wow, yourself," he said, kissing her soft cheeks, seeing how long he could resist her mouth.

The baby awoke and started crying.

Mariella pulled away and hurried over to him.

"Oh, sweetie, what's the matter?" She picked him up and cuddled him.

"He was fussy eating, too," she said. "Maybe he doesn't want to sleep in the stroller. I'll take him home."

"I can drive you."

"No, we'll walk. It's still a pretty day. We'll be okay."

In only a couple of minutes they left.

He watched as she disappeared from view. Whether she knew it or not, the love she showed for the baby was strong. She would love that child forever. Her concerns on whether she was a good mother were for naught. When would she accept that?

He wished he could give her that knowledge.

Mariella pushed the carriage along the side of the road, not seeing the scenery, only halfway watching for vehicles. She was bemused with their kiss, concerned by the baby's fussy behavior. She was smiling, her heart still beating faster than normal, just thinking about Cristiano. She felt they were drawing closer. And he obviously felt that attraction she did, if his kiss was anything to go by. She wished they had not been interrupted.

"Not that you knew you were interrupting," she said to Dante. The baby was awake, fussy, his fist in his mouth.

She hoped Dante would nap in the crib. She wished to turn right around and go back to spend the afternoon with Cristiano. And share a few more blazing kisses.

Cristiano headed for the small shed in the back of the property. He entered, smelling the sawdust and polish. Slowly he relaxed. Whenever he came into the workroom he felt connected to his grandfather. His mother's father had been a craftsman in furniture making. He'd shown Cristiano the basics and had urged him to follow in his footsteps.

Cristiano had rebelled, as youth so often did, preferring the excitement of pitting his skills against that of a roaring conflagration and rescuing people from impossible odds— who would die if he hadn't been there. But always in the back of his mind were the quiet peaceful times he'd worked with his grandfather in this very workspace.

Since recuperating, Cristiano had built several small pieces of furniture. They were lined up against the side wall, polished to a high sheen, as if awaiting being taken home. He thought his grandfather would be pleased if he could see.

He went to the stack of wood against the opposite wall. He looked at each piece, selecting one of fine cherry wood. The overall dimensions were small, but would suffice for a project. Cristiano wanted to build a table and two chairs for Dante. The baby couldn't use a set for a couple of years, but Cristiano liked the idea of making something fine from Lake Clarissa. Once the boy was older, he'd learn of their visit to the lake. And Mariella could tell him of the fire-fighter who'd made him a table.

He put the piece of wood on the worktable, already envisioning the set. Small enough for a toddler, yet sturdy enough to last for years. Mariella would undoubtedly marry at some point—pretty women didn't stay single for long—and have more children. He hesitated a moment when thinking of her with another man. That idea didn't sit well. Unless he licked this hangover from the bombing, there would be nothing he could do about that.

He picked up a pencil and tape measure and began marking the wood for the first cuts.

When the phone rang half an hour later, Cristiano stared at it, debating whether to answer or not. It was most likely his sister or father. It might be Mariella. Though he had not given her the number, the Bertatalis had it. The ringing continued. Whoever was calling wouldn't give up. What had happened to the answering machine? He remembered—he'd unplugged it when hooking his computer to the Internet for Mariella.

Finally he reached for the phone to stop the sound.

*"Ciao?"*

"Finally. I was wondering if you'd ever answer," his sister's voice came cross the line. "How are you?"

"Fine." He leaned against the wall, wondering if he'd made a mistake staying away so long. Still, it was good to hear her voice.

"That's all? Fine. When are you coming here?"

"Why do I need to?"

"To see us. To see Papa. Surely you've recovered from your injuries by now."

"I have." At least the external ones. "But I've been busy."

"Come for dinner tonight."

"I told you I'm busy. I can't come for dinner."

"If not tonight, then later in the week?"

"Maybe." Not.

He heard her exaggerated sigh. "Tell me about your new friend, Mariella," she said unexpectedly. "I liked her."

He remembered their kisses. Swallowing, he hoped his voice came out normal. "She's visiting here, that's all."

"Where did you meet her?"

"I rescued her from a fire. She and the baby."

"She said she'd had the sauce at your house when you gave her lunch one day. That was unexpected. I sent another jar home to you with her."

"I know, thanks." The memory of their lunch surfaced. She had loved the sauce. If they shared a meal again, he'd get to see her delight in the flavor.

"Honestly, Cristiano, getting you to talk is like pulling teeth. Tell me something."

He laughed as a warmth of affection for his sister swept through him. He'd forgotten how much Isabella always wanted to know everything. Her curiosity knew no bounds. He missed her. "She came by to say thank you. I fed her lunch. End of story."

"So you're not going to see her again."

"Of course I am." A prick of panic flared at the thought of not seeing her again. One day soon, she'd return to Rome. But until then, he would see her again.

The surprised silence on the other end extended for several seconds. Then Isabella said, "I'm planning a family reunion at the end of the month. Actually, if you can keep it secret, it's a surprise for Papa."

"What kind of surprise? It's not his birthday." Cristiano was glad it was not a surprise party for him. Why did women want to have those?

"Just a surprise. But I don't want him to suspect, so, if

you're well again, I thought we could say it was a celebration of your recovery. That way he will know about it, but not that it's for him."

"I've been fine for a few weeks now."

"Not that any of us knew. I haven't seen you since you got home from hospital. If you're really okay, come by the restaurant one day. Come to dinner."

"I'll let you know."

"Keep the last Saturday free for the party."

Once he hung up, Cristiano almost groaned. Attending a party was the last thing he wanted. Yet how could he continue to deny his family? He missed them. He was fortunate to have a brother and sister, cousins. An aunt he didn't see much of. Still, maybe he could manage one evening.

He resumed his work on the child's table, thinking about the baby, trying to picture him growing up. The countryside was beautiful here. Maybe they could spend holidays in Lake Clarissa. There were endless acres of forest a young boy could safely explore. Water sports in summer on the lake. He worried Dante might dart into traffic in Rome or wander away and get lost and who would know him to help him home? No wonder Mariella worried—there was a lot to worry about when thinking of raising a child. His admiration rose at her willingness to take on that role.

He finished cutting the pieces by late afternoon, telling himself over and over their future had nothing to do with his. Cleaning up, he headed inside. The balmy fall weather couldn't continue forever. He'd eat his dinner on the patio if it wasn't too cold, watching the last of the sunshine as the shadows of night crossed the lake.

And he'd try to keep his mind off Mariella and the baby.

As he cooked dinner he realized it had been days since he'd had a nightmare or flashback. The night of the fire had been bad, but since then—nothing. Maybe he truly was getting better. Too early to know for sure. He'd gone several days between episodes before.

Still, if he continued this way, he'd make it back.

If not, he had a long, lonely life ahead of him.

Conscious of how fast her vacation time was speeding by, Mariella placed Dante in the stroller the next morning, making sure she had bottles and baby cereal, and headed out. The weather was ominous with dark clouds on the horizon and a breeze that was stronger than before. She hoped it wouldn't rain before she got to the cottage. Surely if it began after she arrived, Cristiano would give her a ride back to the village.

She wore her sweatshirt and jeans and wished when the wind blew that she'd bought a coat. But she had winter clothes back in Rome so had not needed to spend the money. She would have to return home sooner if the weather got worse.

Rounding the bend before the cottage, she shivered. It was growing colder by the minute and the dark clouds building on the horizon indicated it would surely storm before long. Maybe she should have stayed at the guest cottage. But her time with Cristiano was precious.

She reached the house and was disappointed not to find Cristiano sitting on the patio. Not that anyone in their right mind would be sitting out on a day like today, she thought. Knocking on the door, she blew on her hands. Unprotected while pushing the stroller, they were freezing. She checked Dante, and he smiled his grin at her. He was bundled up and felt warm against her fingers. Of course, they were so cold, how could she judge?

She knocked again.

There was no reply. Moving to the window, she peered

inside. The living room was empty; no lights were on even though it was growing darker by the moment. A gust of wind swirled a handful of leaves around, dancing near her, then moving off the patio.

Mariella heard a high whine from a power saw. She pushed the stroller around the cottage and heard the sound again, coming from a small shed at the far back of the cleared area. The stroller was hard to push on the uneven ground, but if Cristiano was there, she needed to find him. It looked as if it would pour down rain at any moment.

She found the door opened. Cristiano stood with his back to it, cutting a piece of wood. Pushing the baby inside, she was glad to be out of the wind. It felt much warmer in the shed, though she didn't see any sign of a heating unit.

She did see lovely pieces of furniture on one side. Cristiano cut another piece of wood and the baby shrieked at the sound.

He stopped suddenly and spun around.

"I didn't know you were here," he said with a frown. Reaching back, he turned off the saw. "Did you drive?"

"No, we walked. I think it's going to rain."

"It's supposed to storm." He took off safety glasses and tossed them on the wood. Walking over, he grinned at Dante.

"Hey, little guy. You warm enough?"

"Of course, I wrapped him well. I have a favor to ask." She had thought up the request on her walk up—to give herself a reason and not look so blatantly as if she couldn't stay away.

"What?" he asked warily, looking at her.

"Nothing dangerous, though I thought firefighters risked their lives daily for people. Are you telling me you wouldn't even do a little favor that does not involve risk of life or limb?"

"I'm waiting to hear what it is." He stood back up and crossed his arms across his chest, watching her.

Dante played happily with the plastic keys he was gnawing on. Mariella stepped around the stroller.

"Friday is Ariana's birthday. I wanted to go to the cemetery and put some flowers on her grave. A quick trip to Rome would enable me to get some winter clothes. Signora Bertatali said she'd watch Dante."

The thought of going with her to Rome made the bile rise in his throat. It was too soon. He wasn't ready. He stepped away, looking through the door, seeing the back of the cottage and the trees beyond. He couldn't see the lake from here. A moment went by. He wasn't flashing back to the subway tunnel. He took a deep breath, testing his reactions. Nothing. He could hear the baby with the keys, see Mariella from the corner of his eye. No flashback, no terror residual from the bombing.

He had to return to Rome sometime. What better than a fleeting visit knowing he could return to the cottage within hours? Maybe he worried for nothing. Maybe the worst was past and he could move on.

He could visit Stephano's grave.

Cristiano had not been able to attend Stephano's funeral. He'd been in hospital. Nor had he attended any of the many services for all the victims he had been unable to save. Rome had been in mourning for weeks. He'd escaped the worst of it drugged for pain and undergoing skin grafting for his burned hand.

He'd pictured it a thousand times, though. Stephano's coffin lowered into the ground. His wife weeping. His parents stunned with the loss of their only son. He drew in a breath, trying to capture the scent of sawdust to ground him in the present.

The faint hint of flowers caught his attention. Mariella's

special scent. He closed his eyes. The image of their kiss sprang to the forefront.

He opened his eyes, turned and looked at her, hungering for another kiss. He was lonely. Self-imposed or not, he didn't like staying away from his family or friends. Only the shame of not being able to handle things kept him isolated.

Until now.

She reached out and touched his arm, her touch light as a butterfly, yet as hot as a flame.

"Will you?" she asked.

He stared at her. He was thinking of kissing her, hugging her close to him, losing himself in her soft sweetness. And she was focused on a cemetery visit.

"All right, I'll go with you. For Dante. You can tell him you weren't the only one to mourn his mother's loss." He hoped he didn't have a flashback while standing by the graves.

A loud rumble of thunder startled them, causing Dante to begin to cry. Mariella rushed to him and lifted him from the stroller.

"There, there, little man, it's okay. Just noisy." She looked out the still opened door.

Rain poured down in torrents. The yard was already growing muddy as the rain splattered the dirt. The light was almost gone, making it as dark as twilight.

Cristiano breathed deeply the fresh, clean rain-laden air. The sky was a dark grey from horizon to horizon. The rain beat down ferociously. Mariella and the baby couldn't return to the village in this. In fact, they'd become soaked just running to his car. They were stuck for as long as the rain came so hard.

She came to his side, the baby settled on her hip and looking around. He gave his grin and lunged toward

Cristiano. He reached out instinctively to grab him and then was surprised when Mariella let go and he held the baby dangling in front of him. Bringing him close to his chest, he felt the light weight and looked at the baby. Dante gazed at him with dark brown eyes, as if studying a curious specimen. Then he grinned and bopped his head against Cristiano's cheek.

He was a goner. Who couldn't love a sweet baby like this?

"Rain," he said, pointing to the downpour.

The baby gurgled and patted Cristiano's cheek. He felt a tightening in his chest.

"His entire life is before him. What do you think he'll do when he grows up?" he asked softly as Dante settled against him to watch the rain.

"He can be anything he wants. I want him happy and healthy. And when he's older I'll tell him all I remember of his mother," she said, leaning against his left side. Cristiano put his arm around her shoulder. For long moments the three of them looked at the storm.

"And his father? What will you tell him about that man?" Cristiano asked.

"Ariana said he had vanished from their life. And the affair had been a mistake. But that, I would never tell their son. I'll just have to say he's gone."

"Do you think he's dead?"

"I have no idea. I had hoped I'd find something on this trip. People could have forgotten even if Ariana had been through here. Lots of tourists visit this area."

"Hmm."

"I hope it doesn't rain Friday," she said. "Cemeteries are sad enough without the heavens weeping as well."

"Well said. It rained on the day of Stephano's funeral. I think Heaven was weeping," Cristiano said slowly. He had never thought about it that way. He would have been weeping had he been at the church.

"Stephano was your friend?"

"My best friend."

"I'm sorry he died."

"He was killed in the bombing. We were on our third rescue foray when the second bomb went off. The roof of the tunnel completely collapsed, killing everyone still beneath it."

Cristiano wanted to step out into the rain, feel the cleansing of the water, feel the coolness, see the sky above him, know he was alive. But he held the baby, so remained sheltered in the doorway. The trust from Dante touched him. The baby knew the adults around him would care for him.

She reached around his waist, hugging him. "How horrible."

"The entire event was horrible."

"But you saved seven lives. If not for you, they would have perished in the second bombing."

"It wasn't enough. There were so many still trapped."

"It's amazing, that's what it is. How can you say it wasn't enough? It was more than anyone expected."

"I should have made sure Stephano was right behind me, not lagging behind—that he had not been in the tunnel when it collapsed. We lost seven men from our station." The anguish penetrated to his core. His duty was to save lives. His chosen way was to fight disasters and rescue people. He hadn't even been able to rescue his best friend.

She offered support the only way possible, her body warmth to chase the chill of torment. If only she could truly heal his sorrow. If only anyone could.

# CHAPTER SEVEN

UNAWARE of the turmoil, the baby happily babbled, reaching out once or twice as if to touch the rain. The air grew chilled, but Cristiano didn't move. The child was well wrapped. He felt like the only warm spot in the world where he rested against Cristiano's chest. That and where Mariella touched him.

The silence extended. Yet it wasn't awkward. Instead, it was—almost healing. He took a breath, trying to let go the ache that plagued him with all the death and destruction.

"So how long were you and Stephano friends?" she asked.

Cristiano almost smiled. "I remember the first day I met him—it was at the training for firefighting. He came from Genoa, a man loving the sea. I came from here—hills and lakes. He was an only child, had a pretty wife and parents who doted on him. We both passionately loved soccer. We were paired up in training and the rest—"

He hadn't thought about those days in all the months since Stephano had died. Now, telling Mariella, he let the memories wash through him. They'd had fun times. They'd fought fires in Rome. Been sent to man the lines in raging forest fires worldwide. Practiced paramedical routines to save lives. And spent a lot of time together in their off hours.

"He was always up for adventure." Slowly Cristiano began to speak of his friend, remembering aloud the trips to the sea, the ski trip that had ended with both falling face first in the snow, and how quickly they'd progressed from that. The quiet times by a fire, sharing philosophies, plans for the future.

"His wife would probably like to hear from you," Mariella said as Cristiano wound down after telling her many of the shared experiences. "You haven't seen her since?"

He shook his head. "How can I face her when I lived and Stephano didn't?"

"You didn't kill him. The terrorists did. You and she have a shared love of the man—different, of course, but bonding nonetheless. I bet she misses you being around."

"I would remind her of Stephano."

"Maybe she wants to be reminded. Maybe she wants someone around who knew him, faults and all. Who can remember the happy times together. Celebrate his life, not ignore it."

"You don't understand."

She shrugged. The baby was growing more and more squirmy.

"He's probably hungry. I'll take him," she said, reaching for Dante.

He relinquished the child, feeling the cold air hit where the baby had been.

"What are you working on?" she asked, moving back to the workbench and looking at the wooden pieces.

Cristiano turned as well. The emotional toll started to overwhelm him. Needing a diversion, he crossed the small room and picked up one of the pieces that would be a chair leg. "A table and chair set for Dante."

"Wow, you can do that? Did you do all those?" She looked at the pieces lined up against the wall.

"It's been a long summer. I don't just ignore housework," he said, trying to lighten the mood.

"These are beautiful." She stroked a finger across the smooth polished top of a small half pie table. The cabriolet legs were elegant. The rich cherry wood gleamed even in the defused lighting.

"Those legs were hard to do. I ruined more pieces than I wanted." Temper had played a part, but he didn't need to tell her that. Impatient with his recovery, feeling helpless, he'd taken it out on the wood.

"And this, what a beauty this is. Did you make it for someone?" The small console table had classic lines and a band of inlay lighter wood in the perimeter.

"Just made them to kill time while recuperating."

"I'd buy this one if it's for sale," she said hesitantly.

"You can have it. No charge." He wondered where she would put it. Could he visit her one day and see how she was using it? It made him think of a connection between them. For as long as she held onto the table, she'd be holding onto a part of him.

He turned back to the workbench.

"Go on and work if you wish. Looks like we're going to be here a while with the rain. We won't get in your way," she said with a smile. "I can't wait to see what Dante's going to get. He's one lucky boy, isn't he?"

That damned optimism. Cristiano shook his head. How could she think that? The kid had no mother or father. No known relatives. He placed a terrible burden on the young woman now his mother. Yet Mariella seemed sincere in her comment.

Cristiano began working on the leg. At first he was conscious of Mariella watching him. But soon the pleasure he took in working with wood took over.

He was aware when she fed the baby, of the soft lullaby after he ate. Then when she put him down in the stroller for nap. She came back to stand beside him.

"Circle of life sort of thing, isn't it?" she said.

"What is?"

"You fight fire and destruction, and now create things of beauty. A balance. Is that why you do it? To balance out?"

"No. I do it because I like it. My grandfather taught me."

"And your father taught you to cook?"

"A bit. I do like good food prepared well."

"I can boil eggs," she said impishly.

He laughed. He couldn't help it. She'd been to America and back. Was capable of taking on an infant. And couldn't cook worth beans?

"So you and Dante will live happily ever after on boiled eggs."

"I might have to expand my repertoire," she said, wrinkling her nose. "Maybe you can give me some hints." She frowned. "You don't think that will be a problem in the future, do you? I mean, I can learn. And for now he's just beginning to eat baby food, so no worries."

"I'm sure that's not a condition of growing up healthy. Though to enjoy eating, you do need to know more than how to boil eggs." He shook his head. All the members of his family knew how to cook. Well, he wasn't sure about the newly found half-brothers from America. But if they lived alone at any time, they would cook for themselves.

"So tell me what you're doing now," she said, pressing closer. She was a toucher. He hadn't been touched since he left hospital. Until now. Every time Mariella came close, she reached out or bumped against him. He liked the human contact. The thought of pulling her into his arms grew stronger by the second.

He cleared his throat and began to explain, hoping talking would get his mind off what his body was craving—contact up close and personal with Mariella Holmes.

The worst of the storm seemed to be easing. The baby slept in the stroller. And Cristiano showed his work to an interested party. Mariella exclaimed over the craftsmanship and he felt the tightness ease. He might not be a hundred per cent yet, but he still had the ability to build something beautiful.

He glanced at his watch, surprised to see the morning had fled.

"I can give you a ride back. The worst of the rain seems over."

"Beats pushing the stroller. Plus it's decidedly colder after the rain."

Once in the car, Cristiano looked at her. "Since we're going out, what about lunch?" He surprised himself, then knew it was the right thing to do when she gave a happy nod.

"I would love that. I'm hungry. Do we have time to go to Monta Correnti? We could eat at your family's restaurant."

Cristiano hesitated. There was Pietro's in the village. He'd much rather eat there. He hadn't been to Rosa since long before the bomb. He felt a moment of panic. What if he had a flashback in the restaurant? What if he completely lost sight of reality and ended up beneath a table? His family would be horrified.

He knew he had to face his family at some time. The longer he delayed, the more suspicious his absence would become. His sister and father already complained they never saw him.

Yet, he wasn't ready.

Would he ever be?

"Never mind. Forget it. Pietro's is fine. Of course their sauce is not as good," she said.

"Fine, we'll go to Rosa." With any luck, his sister would be too busy to stop to talk to him. Though lunch during the week wasn't normally as crowded as dinners—or weekend crowds. With real luck, he'd act normal for the time it took to order and eat. Then get out of Monta Correnti and back to the safety of the cottage.

He drove through the intermittent rain testing his will power. He tried to gauge his feelings as they approached the town his family lived in. So far so good.

As they reached the outskirts of Monta Correnti she spoke for the first time since leaving the village.

"It's really pretty, even in the rain. I can see why Ariana spoke so fondly of it. And the memories I think were happy even though the end of their affair brought pain."

The closer he drove to the restaurant, the more the tension rose. It would be the first time he'd seen Isabella in months. The sporadic phone conversations didn't count. She would have a hundred questions. He'd be trapped until lunch was over. Had he made a mistake coming here?

They parked the car and walked quickly through the rain. Cristiano held a large umbrella he kept stashed in his car. She carried the baby and they moved in step, close together, to avoid the drizzle. It wasn't too late to turn back, he thought as they approached the door. He didn't know how he'd explain the situation to Mariella if he broke down, but he'd come up with something.

Entering the restaurant, Mariella took a deep breath.

"If we could bottle this aroma and pipe it into other

streets, people would flock here," she said. "It makes my mouth water."

Cristiano took a breath. To him it was home, as familiar as ever. The awkward stress grew until he felt it was almost tangible. He could taste the uncertainty and fear. One of the waiters came over. The two men greeted each other.

"We haven't seen you in a long time," the waiter said.

"It has been a while. Is my sister or father in today?"

"No. They are both at some meeting they had to attend."

"We'll sit in the back, if there's room," Cristiano said, letting the relief wash through him. One worry avoided. Now he just had to remain normal until the meal ended.

"Quiet today. Rain keeping people away, I think," the waiter said, leading them back to one of the small tables near the rear wall.

The wooden paneling gave the restaurant a cozy feel, contributing to quiet enjoyment, mixed with anticipation of the meal to come. When the waiter brought the high chair, Mariella strapped Dante in and handed him his plastic keys.

She opened the menu and scanned the offerings. Everything looked delicious. Choosing only one item wasn't easy.

Once they had ordered she leaned back and looked at Cristiano. "Do you know everyone here?"

Cristiano glanced around and shrugged. "I know most of the wait staff and I bet most of the people in the kitchen. My father has owned this place since before I was born."

"Sorry you're missing him today."

Cristiano pushed a glass toward the right a fraction of an inch. "It's just as well."

"Why?" she prodded.

He glanced up. "No reason."

She narrowed her gaze but didn't push the issue.

Breaking a bread stick, she handed half to Dante and began nibbling on the other half. She studied the decor. "When we ate here before we sat on the terrace. It's lovely. I really liked that. Too bad for the rain."

Just then there was a commotion by the door. Cristiano looked over and frowned.

Mariella turned around to see.

A woman in her early sixties was arguing with one of the waiters. She turned as if in a huff and then spotted Cristiano.

"Oh-oh," he said softly even as he began to rise as she stormed over.

"Cristiano." She reached him and kissed both cheeks. "I thought you were injured and recuperating." She ran her gaze from head to toe. "You seem fine to me. You were always such a good-looking boy."

"Aunt Lisa. I am fine."

"Hmm. So I see. Where is your father? What meeting is he attending?"

"I don't know. I expected him to be here."

She looked at Mariella. "How do you do? I'm Lisa Firenzi, Cristiano's aunt."

"Mariella Holmes."

"Holmes? Are you from around here?"

Mariella shook her head. "Rome originally. Most recently, New York."

"Ah, there they have fine restaurants that are appreciated by everyone." She looked around a bit and shook her head. "Cozy. Who wants cozy? Tell your father I want to talk to him. Or your sister. Perhaps Isabella would be easier."

Cristiano smiled slightly. "I'll make sure they know."

She gave a wave and headed back outside.

"Wow, a whirlwind," Mariella said.

"She actually owns the restaurant next door. Even though she's my father's sister, they have barely spoken to each other in years. I wonder what she wants."

"Maybe she appreciates the family she has. I wish I had family somewhere, besides Dante, of course."

"He's lucky to have you. Many people would not consider the child your responsibility. It's such an awesome one."

"Don't you want children?" she asked. "I mean after you marry and all."

He did not want to go there. On the surface, he looked normal. Only he knew what turmoil lurked inside his mind. He could not subject anyone to that. Fearful of what the flashbacks could lead to, he had to make sure no one came in harm's way. How could he enter any kind of intimate relationship with a woman if he could go off the rails without warning?

In fact, it was a risk to be away from the isolation of the cottage for this long.

Not that he'd had a problem since the night of the fire. Twice he'd thought he was coming close, but one look at Mariella and he'd staved off the threatening flashbacks.

For a moment he hoped he was recovering. Maybe he would be able to go back to work before long. It was still too early to say with complete confidence, but he might touch base with his commander in the next week or so.

"Maybe, if I marry," he replied.

"I'm so surprised you didn't go into this business. A ready-made family affair that you could take over when your father retires," Mariella said a short time later when savoring the first bite of her rigatoni. The sauce had a piquant flavor that she relished.

"It's my sister's thing. My brother and I couldn't wait to leave. It always felt too settled here, I guess you'd say."

"So you two chose the opposite extreme. You with your job, he with his races. Why do you both put your lives on the line like that? At least your actions are for some greater good, but just to challenge the laws of physics and risk death in car races seems a bit reckless."

"Ah, but there is that awesome feeling when he succeeds. Can't be measured."

"Is that how you feel about fighting fires?"

"It is always a challenge. No two fires are exactly the same."

"Scary."

He shrugged. He wouldn't admit it, but he had felt fear a few times. Overcoming it to come out on top was another kind of high. One that he could not achieve with the aftermath of the bombing.

"Enough about me and my family. Tell me about New York."

"It's so vibrant. I worked as an usher at theaters to get in to see the shows for free. Spent many rainy or snowy afternoons roaming the museums. I majored in marketing at university. I was not the only non-American in my classes. There were also students from the UK and Japan."

"You would have more chance of a high-paying job if you didn't have the baby."

"My entire life would be different if I didn't have Dante. I was set to partner with a fellow student in New York in a marketing firm."

"Must have been tough to give that up," Cristiano said.

"The reality turns out to be different from my dreams. I love Dante. I am gaining a bit of confidence. It's not forever. When he's in school, I can try something else, use the education I have. There are a lot of single moms out there. They all manage."

"And single fathers, but it still works better if there are two."

She fell silent. A moment later she looked up.

"I'll see if Signora Bertatali can watch Dante when we take a run up to Rome."

He'd take her to the cemetery, then swing by the station and talk to the commander. Check on his own apartment, which had stood empty these last months. He had held onto it with the intent of returning if he could lick the PTSD. And he'd go to see Stephano's widow.

He'd like to see where Mariella and Dante lived, too. He'd take her there to get her clothes. Then they could have dinner on the way back. For the first time in a long while, he felt the stirring of anticipation.

"We'll leave early."

She grinned at him. "How early is early?"

"Seven?"

"Fine. Are you going by the ministry to talk about the award?" she asked.

He'd forgotten about that. He shook his head. "No."

She narrowed her eyes. "Why not?"

"People died in that bombing. Good people. Men who tried to rescue others. I was luckier than most, I got out alive. But there were many more who didn't."

"You saved seven people. Including two children." She reached out to touch his arm. "It must have been terrifying as well as horrific. So many people lost their lives."

Including Stephano. Cristiano began to feel the stirrings of a panic attack. His vision was growing dark around the edges. His heart began pounding in remembered fear.

Her hand slipped into his and he gripped it, focused on her silvery eyes. And that dusting of freckles across her nose. What would it be like to kiss each and every one? She looked like happiness personified. He knew she'd had some hard knocks herself, but they didn't get her down. For a moment he envied her. He'd give anything to turn the clock back. To be the man he once was.

The moment passed. Another. The restaurant came back into focus—people enjoying the good food, the laughter and conversation conveying their pleasure. He drew a deep breath.

"Did you want dessert?" he asked, withdrawing his hand. Mariella was like a lifeline. Was that the clue? Not lock himself away but be with her all the time?

He'd give almost anything to do just that.

They decided against dessert. Soon they headed back to the car, glad the rain had stopped—if only temporarily. The dark clouds showed the storm had not completely passed.

She remained sitting in the car when Cristiano stopped in front of the Bertatalis' home. Dante was asleep in his car seat, the stroller folded in the trunk.

"It's been a nice day despite the rain. Thank you for lunch," she said.

"My pleasure."

"Your family's restaurant is so nice. I really like it. You're lucky to be a part of that, even if you don't work there."

That might change. If he couldn't return to firefighting, what would he do? Join his sister in the restaurant?

No public job. If he got that bad, he would never be able to be certain he wouldn't have another flashback. He gripped his hands on the steering wheel. Better he'd been killed in the bombing instead of injured. No one would ever have known about the reactions he couldn't control.

He would do his best to make sure no one ever found out.

"Thanks again," she said, opening the door.

"I'll get the stroller." Cristiano got out and retrieved the stroller from the trunk while Mariella took Dante, car seat and all, from the car.

The nightmare woke him again. Cristiano came awake amidst terror. He clenched his hands into fists and fought the tattered memory that wouldn't let go. Flinging off the blanket, he rose and went to the window. Breathing hard, he pushed open the window and drank in the cold night air. Gradually he calmed. He hadn't had a nightmare in days. He'd thought, maybe—was he forever doomed to relive the bombing?

He flung on some clothes and went to the kitchen for some coffee. No going back to sleep after that. He glanced around as he waited for the water to boil, feeling frustrated and angry. Noticing the laptop still on the table, he forced himself to remember Mariella using it. He could picture her blonde hair falling forward when she leaned closer to the screen. Her fingers had flown across the keys. Just thinking about her lowered his anxiety level. He almost smiled, wishing he could see her right now.

Of course starting any relationship with a woman he could scare to death if they slept together and he awoke in the throes of a nightmare would be foolish beyond belief. The kettle whistled and he turned to make the coffee. Still, the thought tantalized. She brought sanity into his life, made him hope for more than he had in a long time. He liked being with her. Wanted to know every speck of information about her life, her hopes, her dreams, now that she had a child to raise.

He wanted her in his life. Dared he risk such a chance?

Once he filled his cup, he prowled around the cottage. He considered going to the workshop and continuing with his project, but felt too edgy. Draining the cup, he grabbed the keys to the motorcycle. He'd ride through the remainder of the night and hope to find peace come dawn.

The roads were lonely, scarcely used even in the summer. No traffic. Few residences scattered miles apart. The world seemed different at night. No people. No animals he could see. Just the strip of asphalt illuminated by the headlight, the rest shadows whipping by, undefined vague splotches of black melding together as he increased the speed of the bike.

He made the circuit he'd completed many times before. Slowing as he approached the village, he looked toward the Bertatalis' cottages. The last time he'd done that one had been on fire. No sign of flames tonight. But the cottage Mariella was staying in was lit up; light spilled from every window.

He turned into the lane that led to the cottages. Stopping by hers, he considered his next step. Knock on the door to see if all was well? Would that scare her? A knock in the middle of the night? What if she'd merely fallen asleep with the lights on?

He glanced toward the east. A slight lightening of the darkness. Dawn was not that far away.

He heard the baby cry.

Quickly he went to the door and knocked.

A tearful Mariella and wailing baby opened the door.

"Cristiano, what are you doing here?"

"What's wrong?" he asked, stepping inside.

"He's been crying most of the night. I can't get him to stop. I've checked everything, given him warm milk, but he doesn't even want the bottle. I don't know what to do." With that she burst into tears.

"Here, give me the baby," he said, preferring dealing with a crying child than a woman's tears.

She complied and then wiped her cheeks. "I'll be right back." She fled.

The baby continued to cry and Cristiano juggled him, remembering another baby who had cried. The smoke and cement particles floating in the thick air had only exacerbated his distress. He would never take fresh air for granted again.

He bounced the baby gently. Watching Dante, he took a breath, testing the limits. Nothing but a warm cottage and a crying baby.

"Hey, little man, none of that. You've kept your mamma up all night by the looks of it," he said easily.

The baby scrunched up his face and looked ready to let fly again.

"Now, now, what's wrong?"

Cristiano rested him against his chest, upright so his head was by his own. Slowly he rubbed the baby's head with his cheek.

Dante hiccuped and then stopped crying, swaying back enough to look at Cristiano. His face was wet with tears, his eyes red. But he looked at Cristiano as if examining a wondrous thing.

"That's better. Give your mother a break. People normally sleep at night."

Mariella entered, having washed her face and pulled on a sweatshirt over her nightgown.

"What are you doing up so late at night? People normally sleep. And how did you get him to stop? He's been crying since before midnight!" Mariella peered at the baby. He still looked as if he'd start crying any second, but so far he was distracted by Cristiano.

"I woke early, took a ride."

"It's freezing outside."

He shrugged. Nothing colder than the way he felt after the nightmares.

"Well, I'm glad you did. Do you think he'll feel like going to sleep?" she asked hopefully, worried eyes studying the baby.

"I don't know, but you look like you could keel over without a problem."

She nodded and brushed her hand lightly over Dante's head. "I am *so* tired. But if he can't sleep, neither can I. I think he's teething. It's what the baby books say for this age. He won't eat, won't sleep, I don't know what else to do."

"Take a nap. I'll watch this little guy."

She looked at him.

The hope brimming in her eyes made Cristiano laugh.

"Really?" she said.

He nodded.

She reached up and pulled his head down for a fleeting kiss. "Thanks. I'm so tired I can hardly stand on my feet. Call me if you need anything." With that she turned and went to the bedroom.

Cristiano watched, feeling the soft press of her lips against his. The lurch in his heart had surprised him. Without wanting it, without knowing it, Mariella had captured his heart. He'd give anything to have her kiss him every day. To share the tasks of caring for the baby, of seeing her sleepy and ready for bed. Desire shot through him and he shook his head. He had a cranky baby in his arms, she was dead tired, and all he could think about was her in that bed, alone. How her blonde hair would be spread across the pillow, soft and silky. Her skin would be warm and smooth.

He turned away from the door and his thoughts and he looked at Dante.

"Your mother weaves a spell on men, watch out," he said.

The baby looked as if he was dazed, his head weaving back and forth.

"Okay, let's get comfortable."

He put Dante down on the sofa to shrug out of his jacket. He hadn't even dropped it on the chair before the baby started crying again.

"Hey, none of that. Your mom needs sleep." Cristiano scooped him up and walked him around the small living room. The child was light and warm. Cuddling him gave Cristiano a sense of peace he hadn't had in a long time. He remembered the infant he'd saved. How was he doing these days? Would he ever have even the faintest remembrance of that awful day? He hoped Dante never had anything more difficult to face than teething.

A few minutes later Dante's head fell against his shoulder. Looking at him, Cristiano realized the baby had finally fallen asleep.

He sat on the sofa, careful not to disturb the sleeping child. Rubbing his back slowly, he let the peace of the cottage take hold. If he could bottle this and take it with him, any time a flashback threatened he'd be instantly cured.

Slowly dawn arrived. The baby slept; Cristiano relished the feel of him in his arms. But his thoughts winged to Mariella. He knew she was sleeping, but he wished she'd wake up and come talk with him. They could discuss options to make Dante's teething easier on all concerned. He wish he knew what the future held.

Even more than that, he wished he'd kissed her back when she'd kissed him.

The sun was well up when Mariella came back into the living room. She'd had several hours of much-needed sleep. Stopping in the doorway, she smiled at the sight. Cristiano was sprawled on the sofa, holding Dante. Both were fast asleep. Even in sleep, his arms cradled her son, keeping him safe.

She stared a long time, longings and wishes surging forward. He was a marvelous man. Strong, sincere and capable. Plus sexy to boot. The beginning beard gave him a rakish look. The muscular chest made the baby seem all the smaller—yet well protected and loved.

She went into the adjacent kitchen and quietly prepared coffee. While it brewed, she looked into the refrigerator for breakfast. She'd feed her savior of last night and send him on his way. She didn't want to impose on his time. He'd already helped more than she should have any reason to expect.

Hopefully Dante would sleep most of the day and she could get another nap.

She heard the baby fussing before she finished boiling the eggs she planned for breakfast. She knew she was no cook, but they could have eggs and toast. And coffee. She excelled in coffee.

"Something smells good," Cristiano said when he walked into the kitchen carrying Dante.

"Coffee. And I boiled us each an egg."

He laughed and, as naturally as if they did it all the time, he stepped closer, leaned in and kissed her sweetly on the mouth. Mariella savored the touch, too quickly ended.

"I like boiled eggs," he said a moment later.

Flustered Mariella could only stammer, "And toast. I can do toast."

"A feast indeed."

"Thank you for letting me sleep," she said, stepping away, feeling overwhelmed with the sensations spinning out of control. She wanted to put Dante in his crib and grab Cristiano with both hands. But she had responsibilities.

"Let me take him and feed him," she said.

"I can hold him while you get things ready. But I would take a cup of coffee."

"Done."

They worked together as if they'd done so before. Soon Dante was nursing on his bottle, but still fussy. Mariella encouraged him to eat, conscious of Cristiano only a few feet away. She wished she'd taken more care in dressing, had put on some makeup.

"I wish he could tell me for sure if he's teething. Babies start getting teeth at six months and he's almost that old already," she said as she teased his lips with the nipple. Dante chewed on it for a moment, then sucked some more, then looked as if he would cry.

"Ask Signora Bertatali what she did for her children— she had three," Cristiano suggested.

"Good idea."

When Dante fell asleep, Mariella smiled and kissed him gently. "Let's hope he stays asleep at least long enough for us to eat," she whispered, rising. "I'll put him in the crib."

Cristiano had started the toast when she returned. She quickly put the eggs into cups and set the table she used for dining.

"Best boiled eggs I ever had," Cristiano said.

She laughed. "Sorry, I'm just not a cook. I ate out mostly in New York—everyone seems to, or order in. My mother cooked at home, but I never wanted much to learn. I bet you're a great cook."

"Could be said by some. Not my father, but those not in the restaurant business think I can make some fine dishes," he agreed. Gazing into her eyes, he smiled.

Mariella felt her heart turn over, then begin to race.

"I could cook dinner for us tonight if you like," he said softly.

"I'd love that," she replied, still caught in the gaze of his dark eyes.

They finished breakfast and, by the time Dante woke again, white fluffy clouds dotted the sky. The chance of rain remained high, but for the short term it looked pleasant outside. Mariella fed and bathed Dante while Cristiano sat nearby to watch. They spoke of myriad things, from her favorite restaurants in New York, to his vacations skiing in the Swiss Alps.

"Come back to my place," he said when the baby was dressed for the day and had smeared oatmeal cereal everywhere.

Mariella merely laughed as she cleaned him up again, looking over at Cristiano. "To do what?"

"You can help me make the table and chairs."

"I know nothing about making furniture."

"Sanding doesn't take a lot of previous experience. Come on, it'll get you out of the house. But I can't bring you two on my motorcycle. You'd have to drive yourself."

"Or we can walk there. Dante loves the stroller."

"So I'll see you soon."

She smiled and nodded, glancing out the window again. "We'll be there soon. But if it looks like rain, we'll have to scoot for home. Maybe I can use your computer again. I want to check the status of the one I ordered. If it's already shipped it might be in Rome when we go up."

Cristiano waited until she had Dante bundled up and in the stroller. He took off on the motorcycle while she began to push the stroller up to the cottage. It was noticeably cooler than it had been. Tomorrow they'd zip into Rome. She'd do what she needed and he'd do what he needed and then she'd return to the lake to finish her vacation. She looked forward to spending the day with him without the baby. With just the two of them, and a carefree day, who knew what might happen?

When she reached the cottage, Dante was asleep. Poor thing, he was probably exhausted from being up all night. She went straight to the workshop in back. As she walked closer she could hear the raspy sound of sandpaper against wood. He had already started.

Parking the carriage just inside the doorway, she stepped further into the workshop. Better for Dante to be near the fresh air than one laden with sawdust. If it began to rain, he would be sheltered and she could get to him quickly.

Cristiano glanced up.

Taking a breath, she relished the scent of furniture oil and fresh-cut wood. "I love the way it smells in here."

"Me, too. Are we set for tomorrow?"

"I checked with Signora Bertatali and she said she'd be delighted to watch Dante. I'm looking forward to our drive. She also said it did sound like Dante is teething. She said to give him something cold to chew on, like a cold damp rag or a rubber toy that's been in the freezer."

He nodded, beckoning her over to watch as he continued with the sanding. She stepped closer and peered at the smooth piece that would become a leg.

Reaching out a finger, she rubbed it in the direction of the grain. "It feels like velvet," she murmured. She looked up. Her face was mere inches from Cristiano's. She could breathe the scent of his aftershave lotion. See the crinkles near his eyes from squinting in the sunshine. Feel the heat radiating from his body. Mesmerized, she gazed into his dark eyes, seeing tiny specks of gold near the irises. For an endless moment time seemed suspended.

A moment later Cristiano leaned forward the scant inches that separated them and kissed her. Mariella closed her eyes, relishing the warmth of his mouth on hers, the excitement that rocketed around within her. The way time felt suspended and only the two of them existed. This kiss was perfect: no pulling away, no fretful baby making noise in the background. Just a man and a woman sharing a special moment.

He pulled back, gazing into her eyes for a long moment, then took a breath and looked around—almost as if he weren't sure where he was.

She smiled and reached out to touch the wood again. Maybe she wasn't the only one knocked off her equilibrium by that kiss. She felt almost giddy with delight. The day seemed brighter than before. The colors more vibrant everywhere she looked. Cristiano seemed happier than she'd ever seen him. She loved watching him.

"Then we're set, we leave early in the morning," he said with a smile, his dark eyes gazing directly into hers.

## CHAPTER EIGHT

CRISTIANO picked up some sandpaper and handed it to Mariella. "Rub it along the length of the leg. We want it totally smooth. No splinters for the little fella." His fingers deliberately brushed against hers in handing her the sandpaper. She smiled and nodded, feeling that tingling awareness that sparked whenever Cristiano was around.

Mariella had never done home projects so she was thrilled to be able to assist. She perched on the stool he had vacated and began rubbing the way he showed her. There was something soothing about the long, slow strokes. She couldn't wait to see the finished table and chairs. She'd never helped to build anything before. Glancing around, taking in everything, she would always remember the quiet time spent in this workshop.

Cristiano was focused on the piece he worked. The quiet was complete except for the sound of sandpaper and the rustling of the wind outside the door. She looked outside. It was growing overcast. She rose and checked the baby. He was fast asleep. Touching him, she knew he was warm beneath the fleecy blanket. She looked around. The beauty of autumn in the hills was evident everywhere she looked. Golden leaves, red leaves, and the occasional brown leaf looked a bit dull in the flat light beneath the clouds. She had seen them with the sun shining on them and they'd made her breathless.

Could she be happy in such a quiet setting?

"What do you do all day?" she asked, returning to the worktable.

"What do you mean?"

"It's quiet. Not many shops in the village, no nightlife to speak of. Do you listen to music or watch television?"

He shrugged. "No television broadcast service up here. Sometimes I listen to the news on the radio. I like the silence."

"Your family lives close enough though. How frequently do you visit them?"

"Not often. They have their lives, I have mine—"

"If I had a family who owned a restaurant, I'd eat there at least once a week. The pasta is so delicious and that sauce. Maybe you get tired of it if that's what you've known your whole life."

"I don't get tired of eating there. It's complicated."

"When do you go back to work?"

"Soon."

Dante began to fuss. Mariella dropped the chair leg she was sanding and went to pick up the baby. He rubbed his face and began to cry. She cuddled him close and walked around, rocking him gently.

"Does he need a bottle?" Cristiano asked, coming over.

"I don't know. He should be sleeping longer than this. If you could prepare a bottle, I'll try that. Maybe he's hungry because of being up so late last night."

Cristiano pushed the empty stroller to the kitchen. In only a moment, following Mariella's instructions, he had the bottle warmed for the baby.

Dante did not want the bottle. Taking the nipple, he

sucked for a moment then let out a wail. He pushed the bottle away and cried.

"Oh, honey, don't fret." Mariella held him up against her shoulder, walking around the stone floor. "Do you think it's more than teething?"

"I think your guess about teething is still likely. I remember Stephano's baby when he was teething. You could check with Signora Bertatali again, if you want. After that, if you aren't convinced, we can try the doctor."

She used his phone and checked with the woman again. When she hung up the phone Mariella looked at him. "She said it still sounds like teething. Give him something to chew on—soft so he won't hurt himself, but firm so he can feel it when he bites down. She said the process could go on for weeks or months."

"Oh, great. Do you have a rubber toy we could put in the refrigerator until it gets cold and let him chew on?"

She shook her head, jiggling him as Dante rubbed his face and cried.

"Maybe a cold washcloth?" she asked.

"That I have. I'll be right back."

In less then five minutes, Cristiano had a cold damp washcloth—soaked in ice water for a moment, then wrung out.

When he offered it to Dante the little boy stopped crying long enough to look at Cristiano. He lunged for him.

"Whoa." Surprised, he took the baby. Holding him in one arm, he offered the cloth again, wrapped around his finger. When Dante clamped down on it he smiled.

"He's got some bite. He keeps biting and releasing."

"At least he's stopped crying. Poor baby." Mariella brushed his downy hair. "This goes on for months? I'll never sleep."

"This might calm him down."

But as the afternoon wore on it was obvious to both adults the child had staying power. He chewed on the washcloth, then cried. They'd swap it out for another cold one, and he'd be content for a little while. Cristiano insisted on taking turns with Mariella as they walked the baby, trying to get him comfortable.

Dante drank a bottle, alternating between chewing on the nipple, crying and sucking. Finally, late in the afternoon he fell asleep.

Mariella held him close. "I think we should go home now," she whispered.

"I don't think the sound of our voices will wake him, he's out," Cristiano said. Hearing a noise, he looked at the windows. "It's raining again. Pouring more like. You don't want to take him out in this. Stay."

She looked at the rain. "So you're stuck with us."

He brushed his fingertips down her cheek. "No problem. The worst is behind us. I'll dash out and make sure the workshop is closed up. We can start dinner, eat a bit early and, when the rain stops, I'll drive you back to the cottage."

She nodded. "If this keeps up, I can't go to Rome tomorrow. I can't leave him when he's not one hundred per cent all right. I wanted to visit Ariana's grave on her birthday, but she'd understand I couldn't leave her son."

"Rome will be there whenever we go, no problem. Truth be told, I'm not sure I'm ready."

"Ready for what? Driving to Rome? Does your ankle hurt?"

"No, not that. I'm not sure I'm ready to face Stephano's wife. He had so much to live for. Why was he killed and not me?"

"We don't know why things happen. I'm sure every

family who was affected by that bombing questions why it happened."

"He saved several people before he was caught in the second blast."

"So he's a hero, too."

"Small help to his family now."

"There is comfort in knowing that, Cristiano," she said gently, reaching out to touch his arm. "I can only imagine how devastated his wife must feel, but she and her children can be proud of what he was doing when he was killed. And I know she would love to see you. I love visiting with friends of Ariana's who were close to her those last months when I was still in New York. Talking about her, remembering her hurts—but it also heals. She didn't have such a great life but she loved life. She was optimistic almost to the end."

"At least you had time to prepare."

"One is never prepared. Go to your friend's wife, talk to her of Stephano. You two probably knew him best in the world. She would want that contact."

He looked away, searched the ceiling, wondered how to truly convey the fear that flooded. "It's not that easy."

"No one said it was easy. It's just important."

"He was a good friend."

"So was Ariana. I think special friends are rare. I wonder if I'll ever have another that I feel as close to as I did with her."

He thought about it for a moment. "Probably not. Another friend that's close, I expect, but not as close. Stephano and I shared a strong bond from the training and the fires we fought together. We took holidays together. He and AnnaMaria always included me in family events."

"She must be hurt you haven't contacted her," Mariella said.

"I thought she wouldn't want to be reminded—"

"She'll need you for the memories you share. You can tell Stephano's children about their father. That'll be special for them."

Cristiano hadn't considered that. He missed his friend, but the best way to honor his memory was to make sure he was never forgotten. He hadn't given his friend's wife the attention she deserved. She would have been even more devastated to lose her husband than he had been to lose a friend. How could he have ignored her pain while dealing with his own?

"Cristiano?"

He looked at Mariella. "What?"

"You looked like you were in a trance."

"Just thinking about Stephano's family. I do need to see them."

"Yes. And your own."

"Why do you say that?"

"You're so lucky to have a big family to rally around when things are tough. They are there for you. I think the bombing must have been very hard on them. You need your family. You need people who know you, who love you, to support you no matter what. They are your support group that will never fail."

"Did you know I found out a few months ago that my father had a wife and two sons before he even met my mother? Yet he never told any of his second family about them. So maybe our family isn't as close as I once thought."

Mariella looked astonished. "You're kidding. What happened?"

"I don't know all the details, it all came out when my father and aunt were arguing. Isabella said the first sons live in America, but they have visited the family here, however I've never met them."

"How odd,' Mariella murmured. "How do you feel about that? I can't imagine learning I had siblings at this age. Is that why you aren't spending time with your family while you recover?"

He hesitated, the urge to explain growing stronger by the second. Yet he couldn't bear to see the disappointment in her expression when she realized he couldn't control his own mind. "It's complicated," he repeated.

"How?"

"For one thing, I can't believe my father never told us we had older siblings. Strangers who share our blood. Apparently he lost touch with them. Isabella didn't give a lot of details."

"So you have even more family than you thought. That's so cool."

He looked at her. "You have a most annoying habit of seeing everything through rose-colored glasses. What about my father's lack of trust in this family, his keeping them secret? His ignoring them for many, many years?"

"Maybe you should ask him why," she suggested. "I'd give anything to belong to a large family, to have people who loved me around to help when I need it. Or just to share good times with. What's wrong with being happy about things? Are you a pessimist?"

"No. A realist. Bad things happen to people. Things that can't ever change. Life is not all sunshine."

"True. But for the most part, it's an exciting adventure. There will be tough times, but happy times, as well. We need to search for the happy. Hold onto it as long as we can to balance the other times."

"Are you happy? You lost your friend, your parents, you're saddled with an infant, working at a job that's not what you planned for. No prospects for change in the near future that I can see."

She nodded and smiled at him. "Today I am happy. The baby is sleeping, you are cooking dinner for me, and I'm healthy. Just because I'm not doing what I thought I would be doing career wise right now doesn't mean I won't at some point in life. I've come to realize these last few days that I could never give Dante up. I will still look for his father so he'll know about him, but I don't know if I'll approach him. I need to make sure Dante stays with me. He's so precious."

"Don't you want to get married, have your own family?"

"Dante is my family. And, yes, I'd like to get married some day. But if that's not in the cards, I'm not going to pine away. Do you want to get married?"

He shrugged. "I'll let my brother and sister take care of future generations."

She laughed. "There's more to marriage than having children. I see it as a partnership of two people sharing their lives together. My parents had a great marriage. In a way, much as I wish things had been different, I'm glad they died together. I think either would have been lost without the other. That's the kind of marriage I want if I ever find the right man."

"Wonder if that's what my father thought he was getting—each time. The first wife left him. My mother died young. He's been a single dad most of his life."

"And, what, five kids? That's got to be sort of nice."

Dante fussed again and she went to quiet him down before he could fully wake up. Cristiano continued preparing the meal while the rain ran down the windows. Had his dad regretted the past? Wished he were closer to the grown sons he had in America. Cristiano had never doubted his father's love. But it seemed as if his entire world had gone topsy-turvy and he didn't like it.

"This is a nice place," she said when she had wheeled the stroller into the darkened living room. "Tell me some more about being a kid at the lake."

The rest of the afternoon passed with both sharing memories of happier times when they'd been younger.

Dinner was delicious.

"If you ever decide to give up firefighting, you could get a job cooking anywhere," Mariella commented as she complimented him on the pasta dish.

He looked at her sharply. "Why would I give up firefighting?"

"I don't know. It's not exactly the kind of job you do in your eighties, is it?" She licked her lips.

"No, it's not a job for an old man. But I've years ahead of me before I'm eighty."

She nodded, laughing softly. "I'll say."

Almost as if he knew dinner was finished, Dante began to cry again. He was not easily placated. They tried the cold washcloth for him to chew on. Tried rubbing his gums with their fingers, wincing when he bit hard. But nothing seemed to work.

Mariella fed him again, a hit or miss with him spitting out the nipple more than he drank from it. "I should be going," she said at one point.

"Stay a bit longer. No need for you to have to handle this alone. I can help."

"If this is like last night, you wouldn't get any sleep."

"We'll trade off. If he screams all night long, I'll take him for a while so you can sleep. I don't need much sleep."

"Thanks, but he's my problem."

"Actually, he's your son, not a problem. This situation can be shared. Let me help, Mariella."

She swayed from side to side trying to soothe the baby. "You don't know what you're in for."

"I do. I saw him last night. And today. We'll be fine. Let's try another cold washcloth."

As they took turns holding the baby and walking the floor with him, the hours slowly passed. A little after midnight Mariella gave into Cristiano's suggestion she go lie down in one of the bedrooms and sleep for a little while.

"What about you?"

"I'll be fine. I'll wake you when I need to go to sleep, unless this little guy finally gives in."

She nodded and closed her eyes for a moment. "I'm dead on my feet," she said. "Thanks, Cristiano. Which room?"

"None of the beds are made but mine. But there are fresh sheets and blankets in the closet along the hall."

"I'll make do."

It was almost three when Dante finally nodded off, tears still on his sweet face. Cristiano continued holding him in the large chair they'd been in for the last couple of hours. The child was in such discomfort nothing seemed to work. Now he would escape that by sleep. Cristiano envied him. He'd love to sleep and escape everything. But he never knew if the nightmares would rage or if the night would be restful.

The rain continued. The sound on the roof reminded him of days in the past when he and his brother and sister had to stay inside because of rain and how they'd railed against the weather.

He missed seeing them. Missed being a part of their lives. Valentino had married! He was trying to adapt to knowing his younger brother was married. And his sister, too! Mariella was right, he had a close family who would rally to his aid, if there were anything they could do.

Time and again he returned to wondering about the newly learned-of brothers. Dante lay across his chest. Cristiano brought up the baby blanket to cover him. He'd leave him right where he was for a while. He knew his father must have held those early babies—twins. Had his father planned a future for his sons? How devastated he must have felt when the boys had to go to America.

Had their mother had family to help out? Or had she been a single mother like Mariella? He'd want to share in all his child's growing—seeing him learn to walk, hear the cute sayings he'd come up with, watch as the amazement of learning blossomed on his face. If he ever married, ever had a child.

"What of you, little man? What will you become? Anything you want. A doctor? Maybe an artist.' He felt a pang when he thought of not seeing the baby again after Mariella left.

What of when Mariella left? He hadn't known her for long, but the feelings that had exploded had nothing to do with length of time knowing her. If things had been different, he'd make sure she didn't disappear back in Rome. He'd court her the old-fashioned way—flowers, dancing, long walks where they could talk about their hopes and dreams and fall in love.

Unfortunately, his future was on hold. Maybe gone.

He reached out and turned the lamp to the lowest setting, dimming the light. He'd see if he could doze a bit while Dante slept. Who knew how long he had?

Mariella woke in daylight. For a moment she wasn't sure where she was, then she remembered. Jumping out from beneath the duvet she'd drawn over herself last night, she hurried out to the living room. The house was silent. Where were Cristiano and Dante?

She stopped at the doorway. One lamp was on, giving little illumination. Cristiano was stretched out on the comfortable chair, his long legs straight out, his head resting on the back. Cradled against his chest, the baby was sound asleep, covered by one of his little blankets. Just like yesterday. She could get used to this.

For a long moment Mariella stared, imprinting the image on her mind for all time. She let herself dream for an instant that this was a usual occurrence. She'd be asleep and then awake to find Cristiano with the baby. She'd waken them and they'd spend their days together. And their nights. Dante would not always need extra care. He was good about sleeping through the nights normally.

She went into the kitchen to clean up from dinner and get something started for breakfast. If only coffee.

Then she needed to make plans to return home. Not for a brief trip, but back to their normal lives. She was falling in love with her firefighter and he was not falling for her. She blinked back tears, feeling the pain of disappointment deep inside. She wished he would, but there was an intangible barrier. Every time she thought they were drawing closer, he'd pull back.

What she felt for him went far deeper than any emotions she'd had before. From time to time growing up, she'd thought she was in love. A boy in high school. A young man in New York. But soon the feelings had faded. Knowing Cristiano showed her how pale the emotions before were compared to her feelings for him now. He was strong, generous, helpful. He saved people's lives. He was a hero several times over. And he made her feel so very special.

Which reminded her of the medal ceremony. He should attend. If not for himself, then for the others he spoke about who were heroes but couldn't be there. She wanted the world to know what a true hero he was.

She wondered how she could convince him to attend. Could his family help? She wasn't even sure they knew. To come right out and tell them seemed a breach of confidence, though Cristiano had never told her not to tell anyone.

She still had the letter. From what she'd read, the award was being made—whether Cristiano accepted it in person or not.

The cottage was quiet. Cristiano's computer sat on the table from before. Mariella turned on the computer, surrounded by the warmth of the cottage kitchen, redolent with the fragrance of coffee brewing. She checked messages, contacted her clients to let them know she was on top of things. Then she looked up the award ceremony. There was quite a bit of press about the event, honoring those who had responded to the bombing, both living and dead.

It would be held at the Parlamento addressing both the Senato della Repubblica and the Camera dei Deputati. The Prime Minister himself was presenting the awards.

The ceremony was given by a still-grieving nation doing what it could to honor those who had first responded at great personal risk and sacrifice.

The rain finally ended. She closed the laptop and rose to go to the doorway, opening it a crack and breathing in the fresh air, cool and damp. It raised her spirits. She had been on a fool's errand, trying to locate a man who had never wanted to know he had a son. If he'd left Ariana, she should have taken that as a sign. Longing for family of her own should not have had her going against her friend's wishes, however much Mariella wanted Dante to have an extended family. Her limited attempts to locate anyone who had known Ariana in this area had proved totally futile. Another sign?

She did not regret coming, however. If she hadn't, she never would have met Cristiano.

"Be happy, my love, whatever the future brings you," she whispered to the wind, wishing she dared whisper it to him face to face.

Time to go home.

# CHAPTER NINE

THE phone rang.

"Get that, would you?" Cristiano called from the living room. Mariella hurried to the counter and picked it up.

The woman on the other end was obviously surprised when Mariella answered.

"Who is this?"

"Mariella Holmes." She recognized Cristiano's sister instantly.

"Where is Cristiano?" Isabella asked as soon as Mariella identified herself.

She explained how he was watching the fussy baby. "Hang on, I'll get him for you."

"A moment, please, Mariella. Do you know about the awards ceremony for those who rescued people in the bombing last May?" Isabella asked.

"Yes, I was just reading about it on the Internet, actually."

"You know Cristiano is getting a medal, don't you? Is he still refusing to attend?"

"I believe so." She was hesitant to confirm or deny anything. "You need to talk to him." Mariella hurried into the living room and held out the phone.

"It is your sister." She gently picked up the sleeping

baby and rocked him a bit, walking out of the room. But she could still hear Cristiano's side of the conversation.

He was arguing with his sister.

She knew he felt he'd done nothing extraordinary—it was his job to respond to any emergency. He should have done more at the bombing site. He focused on those who hadn't made it, not the ones he'd saved. Somehow he had to see he'd done more than most and merely because he lived didn't mean he hadn't been willing to give all. He hadn't needed to this time.

She heard an expletive, then silence. She stood by the back door, swaying with the baby. Was Cristiano angry with his sister? More likely just angry—at fate, at the way things had turned out.

She didn't know how long she stood there, but when she heard the car in the driveway a short time later she knew it had been long enough for Isabella to drive from Monta Correnti. Mariella watched as Isabella got out and walked quickly to the house. Her long wavy black hair blew in the wind. Her blue eyes looked stormy.

"Hello," Isabella said when she stepped inside.

"Cristiano is in the living room," Mariella said, wondering if she should leave or stay. "Do you want coffee?" She could put the baby in the stroller and prepare coffee—it would give her something to do.

"Yes, please." Isabella took off her jacket and draped it over the back of a chair, then headed to the living room.

Mariella was soon scooping coffee grounds and listening to the raised voices arguing in the living room. It wasn't anything she had not already heard. Cristiano did not want to accept a medal. He didn't feel he'd done anything special. He kept going on about those who had died.

Finally there was silence. Mariella checked the brewing

coffee and then stepped to the doorway. Brother and sister glared at each other.

"I think, Cristiano," Mariella said softly, "that this is something you have to do."

He began to protest, but she raised her hand. "I'm not finished. I've been thinking about it, and reading about it. It's a way for our country to honor those who went to help. What else can we do? We were not there with you. We did not die like your friends and comrades. We did not see the horror. What we did see was the bravery of the first responders who plunged into the inferno without knowing what they would find, or if they'd make it back out. You did—time and again and you saved seven lives to prove it."

"Stephano—" he began, but she raised her hand again and frowned at him.

"Listen to me! You must accept because of Stephano. He is not there to be awarded. Go and represent him and all those men and women you knew who died. Let our country honor your bravery, your courage and the unselfishness you demonstrated by risking your life to save strangers. Our country needs this, Cristiano. No matter what you think, the rest of us know you are a hero and we want to express our appreciation in a way the entire world will understand."

The anguish in his eyes was beyond her understanding. But she was steadfast in facing him. He needed to do this for himself and for those who had died. The tension stretched. Finally he gave an abrupt nod and turned to stride out the front door. "I'll think about it," was all he said.

"Whew," Isabella said, watching him leave. "Thank you, Mariella. You put it eloquently."

"It's only true. He carries this feeling he failed because his friends died, but he didn't. And I know every single one of the seven he saved will bless him all their days."

They returned to the kitchen to pour the coffee. Sitting at the table, Isabella looked at her for a moment, then said,

"His accepting the medal is an even better excuse to have the party. Dad will never suspect anything else."

"Like what?" Mariella asked, confused.

"What I'm telling you is in confidence. You can't tell anyone," Isabella said, leaning closer, dropping her voice slightly.

Mariella blinked. "Okay."

"My father and my aunt each own a restaurant in Monta Correnti. Many years ago, before I was born even, they were joint owners of Sorella. Then they had a major falling out. Dad left the restaurant to Lisa and started Rosa."

Mariella nodded. Where was this going?

"Economic times have been tough lately, people aren't eating out as much. Both restaurants have taken a hit, especially Rosa. For a while there we thought we'd have to close. One way to carry on is to merge the two and find economy of scale to have them both operated as one. They'd still keep their different menus, but economies can be achieved which would go a long way to turning things around. The restaurants would complement each other and continue to thrive."

"So is merging a problem? Are your aunt and father still feuding?"

"Actually, Dad turned the day-to-day operation of the restaurant over to us—Scarlett and me. I've been talking with my aunt and we've decided this is the best way to handle things. We wanted to surprise my father with this merger. I want a fait accompli. He loves the restaurant. I expect he'll go along with anything that keeps it open— even joining forces with his sister. Plus, there's another situation."

Mariella asked, "What is that?"

"Did Cristiano tell you about our American brothers?"

Mariella nodded slowly.

"I want a way to bring the entire family together—a reunion, if you would. So this is perfect. Everyone loves Cristiano. We've been worried about him these months. To celebrate this honor for him would raise no suspicions. I'll have Alex and Angelo visit from America and I'll make sure Aunt Lisa and her family are present. Then we can mingle, celebrate and announce the plans for the merger. It's perfect!"

"What's perfect?" Cristiano stood in the doorway.

"The excuse for the party I told you about. We'll change it to celebrating the medal."

Cristiano frowned. Isabella ignored him.

"Dad will be so proud of you. We'll have the celebration at the restaurant, of course. Everyone will come." She glanced at her watch. "I've got to go. I'll call you with details." Isabella glanced at Mariella, giving her a wink. "Bring Mariella as well."

When Isabella left, Cristiano sat at the table, looking drained.

"Are you all right?" Mariella asked. "Want some coffee? It's fresh."

He nodded. When he took the cup, he spoke, "There's things you don't know anything about. Other reasons I don't want to accept the medal."

She reached out and took his hand, feeling warmed when he turned to clasp hers. He studied their linked hands for a long moment, then raised his gaze to hers.

"Will you come with me?" he said.

"I can't go." She was stunned. "Someone close to you should go—Isabella or your father."

"You or I don't go at all."

She blinked. "Why me?"

"Because if you're ganging up with Isabella in pressuring me to go, I want you there. I'm sure families are allowed. I'll find out. Otherwise, the deal is off. I don't go."

"Okay, then. I'll go." She would be thrilled to be in the audience when he accepted the medal.

Dante woke and grew fussy. Mariella prepared him a bottle and then had the difficult task of getting him to eat when he was so miserable.

"Can I help?" Cristiano asked, watching them with concern.

"I'm getting the hang of it. You had him earlier."

"There's no time limit. I like that little guy," he said.

She smiled down at the cranky baby and kissed his forehead. "He does grow on you, doesn't he? Go do some woodworking. We'll come out when he's finished eating."

"What makes you think I want to go work?"

"It'll soothe you, you said so—maybe not in so many words, but it shows."

Cristiano went to the shop in back and switched on all the lights. He was in turmoil; the thought of accepting the award not sitting well. And the worry he'd have another flashback in the midst of it all was enough to make him want to flee.

He was sincere in wanting Mariella there. He would look at her, not see in his mind's eye the devastation and horror of that day. He'd focus on her silvery eyes, her optimistic smile, and know he'd risk a hundred forays into hell to see her smile.

"It's an excuse, you know," Mariella said a short time later when she arrived pushing the stroller.

"What is?" He looked up, already feeling better for seeing her and the baby.

"Your medal celebration. Isabella wants a party to announce the merger of Rosa and Sorella."

"What?" He stared at her in stunned surprise. That was the last thing he'd expected to hear.

Quickly she told him what his sister had said.

"And Dad's okay with this?" he asked.

"Apparently it's to be a surprise, but Isabella said he turned things over to her and Scarlett and this is their decision."

"He'll flip."

"Or be proud of yet another offspring—for her business acumen. I still want to talk to her about a mail-order outlet for that sauce. Actually, the place could use a website just to let people know about it. I do have a degree in marketing— maybe I can help."

"Who will be at the party?"

"Just family, and me and Dante. Unless you don't want us to go."

"If I go, you go," he said, pulling her close with his arm around her waist. He leaned in and kissed her.

Wishes do come true, Mariella thought as she savored his kiss, giving back as much as she was able. Maybe she should start wishing for the moon. It could happen he'd fall in love with her, couldn't it? His month moved against hers, leaving to trail kisses across her nose.

"I've wanted to kiss those freckles since I first saw you," he murmured, trailing kisses across her cheek, down to her jaw, lower to the pulse point at the base of her throat, wildly beating as the blood rushed through her. She was floating in delight. Seeking his mouth, she sighed in contentment when he covered hers with his and deepened the kiss.

Long moments later they were both breathing hard. He pulled back a scant inch. "Is the baby okay?"

"I haven't heard him. I'll check."

Cristiano did not loosen his hold.

"Or maybe I'll just listen from here."

He kissed her gently.

"If he makes it through okay today, let's try Rome in the morning," he said. "We missed your friend's birthday, but it'll still be close."

She nodded, still in the circle of his arms, where she'd like to stay forever.

"You'll be okay about the medal?" she asked softly.

He groaned softly and rested his forehead against hers. "We'll just see, won't we?"

"What does that mean? Sometimes you're a bit cryptic."

"We'll just see."

Cristiano didn't want to talk. He wanted to hold her, kiss her, make love to her. His feelings were already entangled with Mariella Holmes. He couldn't take things any farther until he knew if he'd come through this a whole man.

He would never tie anyone to a man who couldn't function in today's world.

The thought seared his brain. He wanted her. He wanted what others had—a life's companion that would share the journey through the years. Share good times and bad, laugh with friends, children. He needed to affirm life, to relish the ordinariness of the day. Take what the day offered and not worry about the future. One day at a time. How far could that take them? Would it be enough?

Cristiano breathed deeply of the fresh, clean country air, the scent of wood and oil. The sun shone from a cloudy sky. The air was crisp and cool after the rain. It was a perfect day. And he vowed he'd spend it with Mariella and the baby. Time was fleeing, he had to make the most of every moment.

They took Dante for a walk in the stroller after lunch to

keep him occupied. Even though he was fussy, the change seemed to work. Cristiano had never imagined he'd be content to walk alongside a woman and baby on a quiet country road. Where was the adventure of Rome, the exciting life he'd demanded before? Stephano had told him how much richer life was married to AnnaMaria. He'd been over the moon when his son had been born, then his daughter.

"You're quiet," Mariella said.

"Thinking about Stephano's son. He's three now. His daughter is almost two."

"Go visit."

"When I drive you to Rome." It would be perfect, time constraints keeping it short. He could handle that. At least he hoped so. Would seeing AnnaMaria bring up all the anguish? Was she missing him as Mariella suggested? Or would she rather he not barge in? It had been six months; maybe she was getting on with her life and didn't need a part of the past.

"I was thinking of returning home. Not just for a quick trip," she said slowly.

That surprised him. "I thought you had some more vacation time."

"I do, or at least less demands on my time until my major clients return. But I'm going to stop trying to find Dante's father. The more I think about what you said, the more I question if I truly want him found. What if he tries to take Dante from me? I couldn't bear that. I used to think it would be okay, his father could tell him about Ariana. But they weren't together for long. And a man who could walk away like that isn't the one I want for a father for Dante. Better he stays with me. Some of my rationale in searching was the fear of being the sole person responsible for this child. But it looks as if that's the way it'll be. I think I can do it. I'll have to, won't I?"

"You'll probably marry some day. Then Dante will have a father. Pick a good one."

She avoided his eyes as they strolled along. Had he touched a nerve?

"Problem?"

"No."

He waited. Mariella usually wasn't so quiet. Something was wrong; even he could figure that out. "What?"

She glanced at him. "Nothing. Just—not many men will want to take on a ready-made family."

"Hmm, wonder if that's what kept my father silent all these years."

"What do you mean?"

"What would you do if you found out your father had been married before your mother, that all your life until you were thirty—well, all your life up to now—you thought you were the oldest of your father's children and suddenly you find out you have two older brothers?"

"I imagine I'd be thrilled. But then I think I have a different take on family than you seem to."

"It's not what it's cracked up to be."

"Why not?

"My grandmother made a mistake a long time ago, resulting in my father. His half-siblings never forgave her or him. It wasn't his fault he was born. But it still split the family. What I remember about my aunt and father was the constant fights and altercations. I know that when Dad hit a bad patch he asked his sister for financial help. She refused. So I should rejoice in finding more family?"

"If your sister asked for help would you refuse?"

"Of course not. I'd do anything for Isabella."

"And your brother?"

"Yes."

"How about your aunt?"

"Never."

She laughed. "Careful, she's going to be even closer tied if the merger goes through."

"That's another thing—what is Isabella thinking of?"

"Maybe of a way to get this split family back together acting like a solid family, with no secrets and no division. Who knows, you might like having older brothers."

"Twins."

She laughed again. "Oh, Cristiano, I wish you'd known them when you were younger. Think of the mischief four of you Casali boys could have gotten into. That would have given your father such joy."

"You have the most annoying habit of being right." He stopped her in the middle of the street and kissed her. "Okay, I'll go to the blasted awards and then Isabella's party and do my best to make nice with strangers, but if the twins start bossing me around—"

She hugged him. "Then you give back as good as you get. My money's on you every time."

The next morning when Mariella walked into the living room after a fitful few hours of sleep, Cristiano was balancing a happy baby.

"Come," he said, beckoning her over.

Taking her hand, he folded three fingers and held her index finger. Gently he rubbed it against Dante's lower jaw.

"A tooth!" she exclaimed. "Oh, baby, you have your first tooth."

"Don't let him bite down, it hurts," Cristiano said, smiling at the baby. "I know."

She opened the baby's mouth. "I can hardly see it."

"It just broke through during the night, I guess. Anyway,

until the next one, I think this kid is going to be back to his normally pleasant baby self."

"I hope I can sleep through the night."

"Me, too."

They grinned at each other.

Then Mariella said, "So I can head for Rome tomorrow. I can never thank you enough for everything. Saving my life—"

"Stop. I told you no debts."

"I know, but still. And helping these last few days with such a cranky baby."

"You sound as if you are saying goodbye."

"I am, sort of. I need to go home."

"Not yet. You have vacation time to finish. Stay, Mariella. Please?"

She hesitated, then wondered if she was thinking clearly when she agreed. "For a little longer." She didn't want to leave—not leave Cristiano behind. But he never mentioned returning to his life in Rome. How long would it take for him to fully recover? Then what? Was staying good or bad? Would she fall even more for the man only to face heartache a few weeks later?

"Today I'll finish the table. Tomorrow we'll go to Rome and take it to your place."

"No rush, it'll be a while before he can use it," she said.

"The table will be done. The chairs a little longer. I like knowing something I've made will be in your home. Maybe you'll think about me from time to time."

She couldn't speak. If he only knew! She loved him. She was going to hate returning home.

"I'll fix coffee," she said with a strangled voice. "And boiled eggs."

"I'll cook breakfast," he said quickly.

Mariella laughed, blinking to keep tears at bay.

The entire time Mariella fed the baby and then ate the delicious eggs Benedict that Cristiano prepared, she felt on the verge of tears. There was nothing to hold her in Lake Clarissa. She had her own life to get back to. But she didn't want to go. She wanted to stay with Cristiano. Was it a good thing he asked her to stay longer? Could they find a future together? Was he even thinking along those lines?

Yet she wanted to hold onto every moment, imprint every second on her mind in case there was not a shared future. The way Cristiano looked by the stove. The smiles he gave the baby, who was in a much better mood today. The way the sun shone on his dark hair when he passed by the window. Taking a deep breath, she smelled his scent, uniquely his. Her heart pounded and she had to take another breath to avoid breaking into tears. She longed for the right to ask him to hold her, kiss her. Make love with her. To be part of his breakfast every morning and sleep with him every night.

Soon after she ate, she insisted on returning to the rental cottage. She needed some breathing room and a serious talk with herself to make sure she didn't give away her feelings. She'd take a few more days' vacation and then return to Rome for good without ever letting him know how much she loved him.

The next morning Mariella kissed the baby goodbye and gave Signora Bertatali a dozen last-minute instructions.

"Go, have a good day. I know how to take care of *bambinos*." The older woman practically shooed her from the house.

Cristiano waited by his dark sleek speed machine. The instant Mariella sat inside she felt carefree and adventurous. She loved Dante to bits, but she was elated to be free of responsibility for a few hours.

It was an awesome car, much more suited to couples than families. And its driver drove as if he were in a grand prix or something. Smoothly taking the curves, accelerating on the straight ways. The ride was exhilarating.

"We'll be there in ten minutes, at this rate," she said.

"Too fast?"

"Not if you can handle it," she replied. For the first time in months she was totally on her own—no baby demanding her every moment. She missed Dante, but knew she'd be back with him in a few hours. She needed the break.

And who better to take it with than the man of her dreams? The car suited her image of him, fast and yet in control. Risking life and limb fighting fires, yet considerate and always looking out for others. He was a caring man and there were few of those around.

"Are you going to see Stephano's wife?" she asked.

"I'll see her once I drop you off at your place after we visit the cemetery."

She looked in the back and the small table wedged in. Reaching back, she ran her fingertips over the satiny wood. "It looks amazing. I can't wait to have it in the apartment. Who else will you see?" she asked. "Are you stopping by the ministry?"

"No. I called them yesterday and got all the information I need for the ceremony," he said. "We have to be there by seven. The actual ceremony begins at eight." He reached out and took her hand. "Wear something very pretty."

"And your family party is the next night. Tell me more about your family. If I'm to meet everyone, I need to know who's who, the relationships and how much you like them—or not," she said.

"What does it matter if I like them or not?"

"No sense wasting my time on people you don't like. I wouldn't like them either."

He laughed and squeezed her hand, then rested it on his thigh. "I don't know the older brothers, but I don't think I'll like them."

"Not fair, you have to meet them first. Who else?"

The rest of the drive was accomplished with Cristiano telling her about his aunt, his cousins, his brother and sister and what little he knew of the unknown men from America.

Reaching the outskirts of Rome, Mariella gave directions to the old cemetery. The visit was brief. Cristiano held back while Mariella went right to the small headstone marking the final resting place of her dearest friend.

He looked around. Stephano was buried in the cemetery closer to his home. He had yet to visit the grave. Maybe soon. But not just yet.

"Thank you. It was important to me," Mariella said when she rejoined him.

He nodded, wishing he could do more to ease her grief. Wishing his own would vanish.

She directed him to the apartment building housing her flat. It was on an older road, stone façade looking weathered and ancient.

He carried up the finished table. Entering, he looked around. "Nice." It was simply furnished, but every item was in good shape. The upholstered pieces looked comfortable. There was enough baby paraphernalia to tell the world a baby lived there, but not too much clutter in the small apartment.

"There, I think?" she said, pointing to a spot beneath the window. "When he's older, he'll have a place to play blocks or color with crayons. I can't wait."

Cristiano wished he could be there to see Dante toddling

around. Running in to tell his mother some exciting news, or bringing some friends over when he was older.

"I'll be ready to go after three," she said.

"I'll pick you up then." He brushed her lips lightly with a kiss and headed out. Time to stop in and see his chief and then go see AnnaMaria.

It was shortly before three when he stopped in front of Mariella's apartment building. The meeting with his captain had gone well. As soon as he received the release from the doctor, he was free to return to work.

AnnaMaria had welcomed him with open arms. Once the initial awkwardness had passed, he'd felt right at home. The only difference was he had expected Stephano to walk in at any moment. AnnaMaria had even commented on that. It helped her through the days, she said, imaging he was just away.

Their son had grown and talked a mile a minute. Cristiano couldn't help thinking of Dante in a few years. He'd be much like Stephano's son. Would the two boys like each other? In another time and place, they might have been friends like him and Stephano. The little girl was napping, but he could see Stephano's features in a feminine version on her face when he peeked in at her.

The afternoon sped by. Cristiano vowed to stay in closer touch with AnnaMaria and told her to call on him for any help she needed. They talked of the future, near and distant, and the fact Stephano was getting a posthumous award and she'd be there to receive it.

Arriving at Mariella's apartment a few minutes earlier than planned, Cristiano thought about waiting before going up—not wanting to appear anxious. "Forget this," he said, climbing out of the car. So he was early. If she wasn't ready to go, he'd wait in her flat. At least he'd be with her. Then they'd drive back, maybe eat dinner at Rosa, show his sister his face so she would be reassured. Talk about their day, make further plans for the award ceremony that he was now resigned to attend.

Mariella greeted him with a smile. "Come in. Want something to drink before we leave?"

"No. I'm not in a hurry."

"How did it go with AnnaMaria?"

He told her a little of the afternoon. "It was odd with Stephano not there. I always think of her with him."

"It must be hard for her."

He nodded.

"I'm almost ready. The new computer is set up. I had a lot of things stored on my backup drive, so could just reload." As she chatted about how she'd spent her afternoon, Cristiano settled in on the sofa, enjoying the normalcy of the moment. Feeling cautiously optimistic he wondered if he dared risk returning to work soon.

And if he dared take this relationship with Mariella another step.

"We could stop for dinner on the way home," he suggested.

"Terrific. In Monta Correnti?"

He nodded.

"Rosa?" she asked.

"Would you like to try Sorella? See the competition my sister wants to merge with?"

"Is it as good?"

"Not the sauce, but my aunt doesn't do anything by halves. No deadline to be home for Dante?"

"I checked with Signora Bertatali about a half-hour ago. He's doing fine."

She finished loading the computer. Shut it down and packed it in its carrying case. "I have this to take and another suitcase of clothes. I'm tired of wearing the few things I bought after the fire. And I have more for Dante. I think he's already outgrowing the clothes I bought last week."

"All set, then."

They headed out to the car. Cristiano placed the suitcase in the trunk, reached to take the computer from Mariella when the wail of sirens filled the air, growing louder by the second. The klaxons sounded at the intersection as two large fire engines roared down the street, the noise amplified between the buildings.

Suddenly the neighborhood vanished. He crouched low as the debris fell. The air was acrid with smoke, so thick he couldn't see two feet in front of him. The baby screamed in his arms, the child he carried whimpered softly, clinging fiercely. "Stephano," he yelled, fighting to keep going. The roof was collapsing. A second bomb had blown. Where were the stairs leading up from the subway station? Searing pain hit his leg, his ankle. He couldn't breathe, couldn't see. His helmet faceplate was broken, smoke and dust surrounded him, blinded him.

The wailing sirens filled his senses, the smoke impossible to see through. Heat scorched from behind from the fire. Concrete rained down. Chaos and confusion reigned. "Stephano?" He yelled again, heard nothing but the roar of the world collapsing around him. He couldn't move. Couldn't go forward, couldn't go back. He had two children to save. Where were his fellow first responders? Was he alone in a world gone mad?

"Cristiano!"

A voice called. It wasn't yelling. He could scarcely hear it over the klaxons echoing from the apartment façades.

"Cristiano, what's happening?"

He recognized that voice. What was Mariella doing in the subway? Had she been trying to catch a train?

"Cristiano, stop, you're scaring me." She shook him, patted his cheeks.

He closed his eyes and the world went black.

# CHAPTER TEN

"CRISTIANO!" Mariella clutched his arm, shaking him again. She was stooped down beside him. When he fell against the car, she looked around. One of the men on the sidewalk hurried over. Panic filled her. What was wrong with him?

"Do you need help?" the man asked, leaning over.

Cristiano opened his eyes and gazed up at them, dazed.

"Yes. He's had a seizure. If I can get him standing, I think I can get him to my apartment," she said. "I can call an ambulance from there."

"No—no ambulance. I need to sit for a minute," Cristiano said, shaking his head as if to clear it.

The man helped Cristiano get to his feet.

"You sure? An ambulance could be here in a few minutes," he asked.

Cristiano nodded, his arm over Mariella's shoulder. "I've had this before. I know how to deal with it. I just need to sit."

*"Grazie,"* Mariella said, leading Cristiano into the apartment building. In only moments they were back in her apartment.

"I'll be okay," he said, still leaning slightly on her.

"Good. Sit on the sofa. I'll make some tea. Do you need to see a doctor? You scared me half to death."

"I don't need any doctor." He sank onto the sofa, elbows on his knees as he dropped his head into his hands.

"You scared me. Are you sure you'll be all right?"

"I'm sure," he said, his voice muffled.

Mariella watched him for a moment, biting her lip in indecision. Finally she headed for her kitchen. "Wait here, I'll make some tea."

She hurried into the kitchen, the initial fear fading. What had happened down there? It was as if he'd spaced out, ducking and yelling. She peeked back to the living room. He hadn't moved.

It seemed to take forever for the water to boil. As soon as she had the tea ready, she hurried back.

He still hadn't moved.

She placed both cups of tea on the coffee table and reached out to touch his shoulder.

He shrugged off her touch, rose and paced to the window. Gazing out, he still seemed dazed.

"Sorry about that," he said with some effort.

"Post-traumatic stress disorder," she said, picking up her cup to take a sip. Wanting her hands to have something to hold since he wasn't letting her hold him.

He swung around. "What do you know about it?"

"You forget, I spent the last four years in New York. America is home to PTSD. The terrorist attacks, hurricanes, major forest fires, earthquakes. Between first responders and the military, there are a lot of people suffering from PTSD. I have a friend whose brother was in Iraq and suffers from it daily. It can be quite debilitating. Is that what you have?"

He nodded. "Now you see why I am not a hero," he said,

turning to gaze back out the window at the scene on the street.

"What does that have to do with anything? You are a hero. Even more so, rescuing me and Dante after what you went through in May." She rose and crossed the room to stand beside him. Reached out to touch him, wanting contact; she wasn't going anywhere.

"Cristiano, you are a hero."

He hit his forehead with the palm of his hand. "Except I'm not right in the head."

She shook him slightly. "My friend calls her brother whacko, but loves him to bits. He does the same thing, goes off into the horror none of us can share."

"I can't get the images out of my head. I wake in the night. Sometimes during the day, out of the blue, I'm suddenly back in that hell. What kind of man does that make me?"

"Human."

He glanced at her, looked back out the window.

"Truly, I don't think we were designed to witness the horrors of modern life. The human mind can only absorb so much. Then it kicks in its defense mechanisms," she said.

"What are mine? Reliving the day forever? It's like I'm stuck in some repeat loop—the smoke, fire, crashing concrete, cries of the dying."

She hugged him, leaning slightly against him until he lifted his arm and put it around her shoulders. "I don't know that much about it. I've heard it can get better with counseling. Sometimes not. There are Vietnam War survivors still suffering from it forty years later. It's an awful payback for being heroic, for doing your best for others. I don't know how you can get over it. Maybe you never will, but it does not diminish who you are or what you've done."

"If I can't function in the world, they might as well lock me up and throw away the key," he said, letting his frustration show.

"Wait a minute—is this the reason you've become a recluse in Lake Clarissa? Does your family know?"

He turned and gripped her shoulders hard. "Do not tell them—do you understand?"

"Why not? It's nothing to be ashamed of. It's not something you can predict, or cure. It's not even something you caused."

"They think of me as some fearless, reckless adrenalin junkie. Daring danger in the line of work. I don't want them to know what a pitiful creature I've become."

"You are not the least pitiful. You are strong, brave, courageous and dependable." She gripped his wrists and shook him as much as she was able. "Pay attention, Cristiano, this isn't your fault. You are a fine man."

"Sure, like just now. Sirens go off and I'm a puddle on the pavement."

"A trigger, right? You heard them and flashed back to that day. From what I read on the Internet, it was horrible. You saw things you'll never forget, terrible things. People dying you couldn't save. Your own friends dying. You were almost killed yourself. Why wouldn't that bother you? You would be a very cold person if it didn't affect you."

"I can't get past it. It's been months. I need to get back to work. But I'm afraid that'll never happen. I ride the trucks that have the sirens. What good would I be if I have a flashback and put others in danger because I can't control what I see?"

Mariella didn't know what to say. Her heart ached for the burden he bore. She could tell by the anguish in his expression that this was something he'd been dealing with since May—alone. She encircled his waist with her arms.

For a moment he held himself rigid, then brought his arms around her. Clinging almost desperately.

"Your ankle was broken when the second bomb went off, wasn't it?" she asked, hoping she was going along the right track. She wished she knew more about PTSD, what triggered it, what might avoid an attack. How people moved beyond it.

"Yes."

"And it healed, but it took time. So, look at it as if your mind got bruised or something. It will take time but it will heal." She prayed she was right. She knew some men never got over the horrors they'd experienced. She hoped Cristiano wasn't one of them. But a man needed hope. She needed him to know that anything was possible.

"Have you seen a counselor?" she asked.

He shook his head. "The doctor at the hospital recommended one, but I left for Lake Clarissa as soon as I was out. There aren't any there."

"Monta Correnti?"

He shrugged.

"There's no shame in being injured," she said gently.

"There's shame when a man wants to be productive and dare not risk going among other people in case something like today happens. What good would I be anywhere? What if I'd been driving? I can't be a risk to others. I was a fool to leave Lake Clarissa today, to hope because I haven't had an episode recently that I was cured. To wish for a normal life like others. It isn't going to happen."

"You don't know that."

"I know I want what I had before—life that was carefree and suited me perfectly. Stephano and his family. My own family. The hope of falling in love and getting married. What of all that?"

"You can still fall in love and get married," she said.

"You still have your family and Stephano's wife and children."

"What woman would want to take on someone like me?" he bit out.

She stared at him. "I would," she said softly. Her heart ached for him. All the more painful for feeling his pain, his frustration when she had so much love to offer.

"Now you sound as crazy as I am," he said. Despite the words, he tightened his embrace and rested his head against hers, holding her firmly against him.

"Neither of us is crazy," she said, her voice muffled against his shoulder.

"If I weren't I'd court you like I were crazy," he said softly.

Her heart skipped a beat and then raced. "Don't play with me, mister," she warned.

He laughed. "I can't offer you anything. I will always cherish the days we spent together at the lake. But you need someone who's whole and free of flashbacks that could wind up injuring you or your son. I wish things were different, but they're not."

"So that's it? You are withdrawing from the world because everything is not perfect in your world?" She pulled back and glared at him.

"It has to be that way."

"No, it doesn't," she said, pushing free from his embrace. "You aren't the type of man to give up easily. Do you love me, Cristiano?"

"I have no right—"

"That's not what I asked." She glared at him. This certainly was not the way she'd expected to find out a man loved her. She had thought of roses and fine dining and dancing.

He took a deep breath, studying her face as if memorizing

it for all time. "I love you, Mariella Holmes. Your sunny disposition brightens my life. Your laughter makes my heart sing. Your devotion to your friend's son is heartwarming. I want you in the worst way—to spend nights in loving you, days in keeping you happy. But I have nothing to offer. I don't have a job I can go back to yet. I don't have the coping skills to make it with PTSD. I'm a mess."

She smiled at him and stepped closer. "I love you, too, Cristiano. I thought the way you were always pushing me away meant that you didn't care for me. But you do. Together we can face anything!"

"Didn't you hear me? There's no future together!"

"I'm ignoring what I don't want to hear. We can manage this. We can. I love you for who you are. I never knew you before, so this suits me perfectly."

"And if I have another meltdown like a little while ago?"

"Then we'll deal with it. Maybe you can start counseling to see if that helps. You can't be the only man from that day suffering from this. Who have you talked to about it? Who have you told?"

"No one."

She shook her head in exasperation. "I pictured you a fighter."

"I am. When there is something I can fight. This—I have no resources."

"So go find out all you can, find the resources to deal with it. Call your captain and tell him. Ask who else is having this problem and what they're doing about it. Oh, Cristiano, don't throw away what we could have together for some misguided notion you are in this alone. Your family would rally around in an instant. Your friends. Everyone. Me especially."

"I can't deal with it."

"Yes, you can. We can."

The silence stretched out for endless moments, then, with a soft sigh, he pulled her into his arms and kissed her. "What did I ever do to deserve this?" he said softly.

Sometime later he rested his forehead against hers and said, "It's not what I want for you. You should have a healthy, perfect man. You'd be getting damaged goods."

"How would I be getting that?" she asked saucily.

"I love you, sweetheart. Would you think—in the future, after we know more about this PTSD and what the prognosis is—would you consider marrying me?"

"Yes! And I don't need to wait for anything. I love you, Cristiano. I want to be with you always. No matter what, we can face it together. Besides, I come with baggage. Dante will need a father."

"Another thing that couldn't be better. I love that little boy. I want to see him grow up, see what kind of man he becomes. And have a part in that, showing him right from wrong, watching him discover the world."

"What better for him than a hero? Remember, you saved his life, it belongs to you."

"His biological father is a fool. I'd be honored to be Dante's father. So you'll marry me? As soon as we know—"

She put her fingertips over his lips. "As soon as we want. We're not waiting for some nebulous time in the future when you decide the stars align right or something. I want to be with you now, starting our memories and traditions. And helping if I can until you lick this thing."

"I have no job."

"I do. If we can live at the cottage for a while, we can manage. Don't say you don't want me unless everything is perfect. Love isn't like that. It takes good and bad, ups and downs. Now that I know you love me, I don't want to be apart. I'm alone in the world except for Dante. With you, I feel whole, complete, part of a family."

"What if I don't get better?"

"Cristiano, what would you do if I got sick?"

"I'd take care of you."

"Yet you want to deprive me of the same opportunity? I want to love you, be with you. Cristiano, that was a proposal and my answer is yes. Not yes someday, plain old yes!"

Her heart sang when he lifted her up to spin her around. "I love you!" he shouted.

She shrieked with mock fear as he spun them both around. "I love you!" she shouted back, then laughed with joy.

They spent the rest of the afternoon kissing, making plans, kissing, calling Cristiano's chief, kissing, and finally departed to return to Lake Clarissa.

"I can't wait to tell Dante," she said as she drove through the streets of Rome. Cristiano had insisted she drive, fearful of another episode if a siren sounded.

"He's six months old, what will he understand?"

"That you're going to be his daddy. That's so special."

"I think it's even more special that you're going to be my wife."

"Will your family approve? When will you tell them?"

He groaned. "Do you know every one of my cousins and siblings got married or engaged in the last six months. Must be something in the water."

"You're kidding!"

"Hey, we're all about the same age, natural, I guess. Only I didn't think I'd find anyone—especially after last May."

"So we can tell them at the party."

"After today I don't know if I should go. What if—?"

"Hey, they'll understand if something happens. You can't cut yourself off from the world. They'll be so proud of you receiving that medal."

"Oh, God," he groaned. "I can't go there."

"Of course you can go. I've known you for weeks and this is the first time I've seen you have a flashback. As long as there are no sirens, you'll probably be fine, don't you think?"

"What I think is if I can just look at you the entire time, I'll be able to do anything," he said, lifting her hand from the wheel and kissing the palm, then replacing it.

"Do you think your family will like me?"

"Yes."

She glanced at him. "That was positive."

"How could they not? You are adorable."

She laughed. "Keep that thought in mind forever."

"That's how long I'll love you. Forever."

# CHAPTER ELEVEN

MARIELLA was dressed in a long gown, a rich dark burgundy velvet, suitable for the most formal of events. Her hair had been done up. Her nails polished to match the gown. She felt the butterflies in her stomach and knew Cristiano had to feel even more stress.

He was picking her up in another ten minutes. She had prayed all week that no sirens would mar the night. She so needed her man to receive his medal, to stand with those who had served beside him in rescuing all they could possibly save. And to stand in place of those comrades who had fallen and were only present in the memories of the minds of those present.

Promptly at the appointed time he knocked on her door. Her downstairs neighbor was watching Dante tonight. Nothing would interfere with the ceremony he so richly deserved.

She opened the door and exclaimed at how handsome he looked in his dress uniform.

"Wow, I'd want you to save me from all burning buildings," she said, leaning forward for his welcomed kiss. She'd only been alone for a day, but she had missed him as much as if they'd been parted a week or longer.

"Don't know if I ever will be able to do that," he murmured, pulling back to look at her. "You are beautiful."

The warm glow seeped through her. She hoped he always thought so.

"I'm ready," she said, reaching for her coat.

"That makes one of us," he said wryly.

"You'll do fine."

"If I end up a puddle on the floor, you'll be to blame."

She squeezed his arm, wishing she could take away every bit of turmoil and uncertainty. Wishing she could make him whole again. Perhaps time would do so, but not tonight.

Tonight was about Cristiano and Stephano and all the others, alive and dead, who had experienced the horror of the bombing together.

He'd hired a limo for the occasion and it was waiting outside her apartment. In only moments they arrived at the Parlamento building, brightly lighted for tonight's event. Reporters and cameramen flanked the cordoned-off entry, calling for sound bites and taking photos and videos of all entering.

"AnnaMaria will be there?" she asked as the limo stopped and Cristiano began to open the door.

"Yes. Her parents and Stephano's will be with her." He stepped out amidst the flashing lights and demands for tell-us-how-you-feel, coming from all directions.

"I probably should not confess to live cameras that I feel like I might throw up, hmm?" he said softly for her ear only.

She laughed and then smiled at the reporters. "I'm so proud to be here with you."

"Then let's walk tall and remember the fallen," he said, offering his arm and escorting her inside.

The buzz from outside was muted once inside the impressive building. Escorts took them to the Senato chamber where Cristiano moved to stand with other recipients while

Mariella was escorted to a seat in the second row. She saw him clearly when he walked in with the others, tall and proud. He looked amazing.

The actual event was full of pomp and ceremony. Television cameras captured everything. The national anthem was played. The Prime Minister spoke about the horror of the day, the attack on a country who had never anticipated such a cowardly assault, the great debt of gratitude the country had for those who had first gone in.

Mariella looked at Cristiano; his gaze was fixed on hers. She tried to relax, to be there for him as a means to hold on and not give way to the fear that plagued him. His eyes did not waver. She hoped he felt at ease.

The names of the men, women and children in the subway trains who perished were read. Relatives and friends sat in the audience. Mariella could hear quiet sobs as names were spoken.

The names of the first responders were then read, each one present stepping forward to receive their country's highest medal for bravery and service above and beyond the call of duty. She clapped wildly when Cristiano's name was called, when he stepped proudly forward to receive the medallion on a banner of Italian colors, green, white and red. He bowed slightly toward Mariella when he received them, his eyes glittering.

She was so proud he loved her. She wanted to stand up and tell the world that brave man had chosen her for his wife. But she merely clapped until her hands were red and stinging, and smiled as broadly as she could.

Then the names of the fallen responders were read. Mariella blotted tears at the moving ceremony, her heart aching for those men and women who had plunged into hell to save and ended up giving their lives. How fortunate their country was to have such brave people.

When the ceremony was over, everyone was invited to a reception. Cristiano found her as soon as the broadcast portion ended.

"Let's get out of here," he said, running his finger around his collar.

"No, first we go to the reception. Those you saved will be there. You must see them. For them to thank you and for you to know you did a miraculous thing that day."

"I don't want thanks."

"Sometimes you have to accept so others can give it. They need closure, too, Cristiano. Don't deny them that."

He drew in a deep breath.

"Very well, but we're not staying long."

The large reception hall was not crowded, though there seemed to be several hundred people present. Mariella met AnnaMaria and conveyed her sorrow on the loss of her husband. People came to congratulate Cristiano, to slap him on the back and some to give hugs. When a man came forward carrying a baby, Mariella watched closely. The child wasn't too much older than Dante.

"You gave me my son," the man said, reaching out to grasp Cristiano's hand. "How you managed I'll never know. I lost my wife, but I have my son, the best part of her. Thank you."

Cristiano smiled at the baby. "He doesn't look any worse for his ordeal. I'm glad."

A young boy came over, looking wary and overwhelmed. His grandparents were with him. "This is Emelio, the last one brought out—with the baby. He is our pride and joy, thank you," they said. "Our daughter and her husband perished, but we have our grandson."

"Thank you for saving me," the little boy said, grinning when Cristiano raised his hand in a high five, slapping it hard.

The young woman he'd first carried came over to thank him, and introduce him to her husband and daughter, both delighted to meet Cristiano and add their thanks.

So went the evening until everyone had greeted the man who had saved their lives.

"Tell me now you don't think you're a hero," Mariella said softly when the last man limped away.

"I was just doing my job. I wish I could have brought more out."

"I know. I think we could leave now," she said. She was exhausted with the emotions of the evening. How much more so must Cristiano be?

They found AnnaMaria and the rest of Stephano's family and said goodbye, with promises to get in touch when they returned to Rome.

Finally they were in the quiet of the limo, speeding through darkened streets.

Mariella squeezed his hand. "You did it, no episode at all!"

"Luck."

"Good luck, then," she said, snuggling close to him.

"I couldn't have done it without you, you know that."

"So we make a good team. I love you," she said.

"Not as much as I love you," he said, leaning over to kiss her.

Just one night later Cristiano parked his car near the piazza in Monta Correnti.

"I'm nervous," Mariella said, looking at the lights over the restaurants.

"We don't have to attend," Cristiano said as he switched off the engine and turned to look at her.

"Yes, we do," she said promptly. "Though if you felt

like this when we went to the medal ceremony, you're even more a hero than I thought."

He reached for her hand and kissed her fingers. "I'd just as soon forget the entire situation and go back to the cottage. You, me and Dante. It's cold enough for a fire, we could sit and talk until he's asleep and then make plans."

It was tempting. But she had to meet the rest of his family some time and maybe it would be better all at once. She had memorized all the names and tried to keep the relationships straight. Plus she didn't want to disappoint his sister. She had worked hard to make sure everyone was there.

"The timing is perfect. We need to let your family celebrate. Besides, remember, this entire gathering is really for your father, the medal award is the excuse."

"I know, but we'll still get more attention than I want now." He took a deep breath. "I hope you're right about their understanding."

"Oh, Cristiano, of course they'll understand. They all love you. If one of them was hurt, you'd be the first there to help. Let them have that same privilege."

"It's not quite as visible as a broken ankle."

"But just as real."

Mariella still marveled that this dynamic man loved her. They had made plans for a quiet wedding before Christmas. For the foreseeable future things would continue much as they had been: she'd work her virtual-assistant job, Cristiano would make furniture—and see a counselor to help him cope with the PTSD. They were very hopeful in time he'd be able to return to Rome and his job. It might take a few months or maybe even a year or so. And if not, he had his woodworking, which he enjoyed. Mariella was convinced he could name his price for the fine pieces he made.

Mostly she was just glad he had not held firm on waiting

to get married until he thought he was cured. She couldn't wait to be his wife, spend her days and nights with him.

"Let's do it, then," he said, opening the car door. They took the baby carrier, though Mariella carried Dante. They'd use the carrier when Dante needed to rest.

In only a moment they were walking into the wide piazza that led to the restaurant. The large stone patio between the two restaurants was illuminated by soft lighting. The chairs were all empty as it was far too cold to sit out at night in November. The front doors of both establishments had prominent signs declaring they were closed for a private party. Mariella heard the voices from Rosa and felt a touch of panic. What if the family didn't want him to marry her? What if he changed his mind? Shaking her head impatiently, she knew she was acting stupid. As if anyone in the family could tell Cristiano what to do. She looked at him for support. She loved him so much she could scarcely believe it. And he loved her! That was the most amazing thing. She'd been deliriously happy these last weeks. And knew once married she'd be even happier. She would have her family—Cristiano and Dante. And maybe a few more babies. But if not, she would feel her world complete.

"Ready?" she asked with a smile.

"As I'll ever be."

With that he opened the door to his father's restaurant and the three of them entered.

"Feels like home," he murmured as they walked into the main room. The tile floor, warm wooden trim and fall colors in the decor were so familiar.

They were immediately spotted by his brother, standing with a small group on one side.

"The hero of the hour!" Valentino called, raising a glass in his honor.

Cristiano looked around. "I don't recognize half these

people. I thought Isabella said it was family," he murmured as he spotted his sister.

"About time. I was worried you wouldn't come," Isabella said, rushing over to give him a hug. "You haven't exactly been a frequent visitor since you started staying in Lake Clarissa." Then she hugged Mariella and Dante. "Welcome. We saw the presentation of the medals on the television. I cried through almost all of it. You looked so tall, so distinguished. I'm proud of you, Cristiano. It's not every day we have a hero in our midst."

Mariella saw him wince and stepped closer. "You've had him all along, maybe you just didn't recognize he was such a hero."

"Well said," Valentino said, giving Cristiano a bear hug as others crowded around, calling greetings. "You remember Clara," he said, reaching for the pretty woman at his side. The love shining from Valentino's face was obvious to the world.

"I remember you," Cristiano said. "Congratulations on marrying this guy. I hope he treats you right. If not, you let me know."

"Oh, he treats me really fine," she said. Rubbing her stomach, she smiled. "The truth will be seeing how he does when the baby comes."

"Congratulations, I didn't know," Cristiano said, shaking his brother's hand and slapping him on the back. "Beat you in the family department, though," he said with a smile at Dante.

"*Ciao*, Cristiano," another voice said.

"Scarlett, I haven't seen you in a while." He smiled at his cousin, and put his arm around Mariella's shoulders. "I'd like everyone to meet Mariella Holmes. My fiancée," he said proudly.

The exclamations and congratulations flew back and forth.

"We have news ourselves," his cousin Lizzie said, coming up to him. He hadn't seen her in years. She was glowing.

"You have new cousins you haven't met yet," she said, giving him a warm welcome. "They're sleeping right over there." She pointed to a double stroller sheltered in the one of the corners of the room, away from the main activity, but close by.

"Twins?" he asked.

"Yes. Must run in the family."

She gave him a hug and laughed. "You haven't seen anyone in a while from what I hear. Glad to see you made it out from that attack with only a broken ankle. That was horrible, for all of us."

The others greeted him, met Mariella and exclaimed in delight over Dante. The baby smiled his one-toothed grin and was soon being passed around as everyone seemed to want to hold the happy baby.

Then Cristiano looked across the room, seeing his half-brothers for the first time. The twins stood near each other, each with a beautiful woman beside him. They looked like their mutual father—only with lighter hair and lighter eyes. Almost as if it had been choreographed, the others parted as Cristiano and Mariella walked across the tiled floor to the two men.

"I'm Cristiano," he said, hesitating only a moment before putting out his hand.

"Angelo," the one with the blue eyes said, reaching out to shake his hand.

"Alex," the more muscular one said.

"Here's Aunt Lisa," his sister said, tugging on his sleeve. "We'll have lots of time tonight to catch up on everything.

Dad should be here soon. We're having drinks and appetizers here, then dinner will be at Sorella. Fingers crossed Dad accepts the merger."

"You can wrap him around your little finger. He'll be pleased things are going to continue, no matter how that happens."

He stepped back a bit and pulled Mariella closer.

"This is more than I expected. Everyone is either engaged or newly married, so we've just doubled the family. But I didn't realize they'd all be here tonight."

"A tribute to you and to your father," Mariella said.

Luca Casali entered the restaurant and greetings were called again. He made the rounds, clasping hands, hugging, getting kissed by most of the women. He looked pleased to see his American sons. Cristiano felt a twinge of uncertainty. He'd always been the older brother. Now he had two older than he. Still, he rejoiced for his father to finally connect with those children he'd had to give up so long ago. He glanced at Dante, being held by his cousin Jackie, and knew it would devastate him if he had to give up the child and never know if he'd see him again. He loved that little baby. He would be the best father he could be for him.

"Son," Luca said, reaching Cristiano. He gave him a big hug. "You have done us all proud," he exclaimed, smiling broadly. "Who knew those fearless escapades when you and Valentino were little would push you to become a man who does such daring rescues? I'm glad you came home to heal and hope you'll visit often after your return to Rome."

"There's something to talk about, Dad, but not here or now. I'm not going back right away."

"Good, I hope we see more of you than we have recently."

"From the looks of things, everyone has had plenty to keep them occupied."

"Luca." His sister Lisa came over. "So, we are united tonight as we have not been in many years. I think Mamma would be happy."

He nodded, glancing around. "I'm sure of it. All her grandchildren here, each with the one special person who will share life's journey with them. It is a happy day. And for me, especially to see my first sons again after so long."

"Attention." Isabella raised her voice above the conversations. Everyone stopped talking and looked at her. Smiles broke out. Glances to Luca were made, then back to Isabella.

"First, I'm so glad everyone could attend tonight. It means a lot to me and, I know, to my father." She smiled at him.

"We are gathered to celebrate my brother receiving a medal from the ministry for his heroic actions after the bombing last May. He was injured in the last moments, yet still managed to keep the children he carried safe and rescued a total of seven people. He also rescued Mariella and Dante from a fire at Lake Clarissa. And that sure had a happy ending."

Everyone laughed, Cristiano with them, leaning down to kiss Mariella quickly. He still had moments of doubt he was doing right by her, but her love was steadfast and he couldn't bear to turn his back on all she offered. He would always do his best to keep her safe and happy.

"But there is another reason we are gathered. Many years ago, my aunt Lisa and my father were left a restaurant by their mother, our grandmother Rosa. They ran it together for a while, then they parted. Different restaurants, different cuisine. Same family, however, though going in different directions. Now we come full circle."

All eyes turned to Luca. Cristiano hoped his father would be pleased.

"We are merging the two back. We will keep the differences in decor and menus, to attract a wide variety of patrons. But Rosa and Sorella will be operated as one unit. Dad, we do this for you. No one could have been a better father given all the setbacks and hardships you faced. This is our thanks to you."

Luca looked stunned. He looked at his sister, surprised to see her smiling.

"I don't know what to say," he said a moment later when no one else spoke. "I can't believe it. It's what Mamma wanted. After all these years—"

Lisa nodded. "You can blame me. I was at fault over a lot. But here's to good fortune for the family from today forward," she said, raising a glass of champagne high.

"Hear, hear."

Each raised a glass to join the toast and drank. Then laughter and conversations started again.

Cristiano walked to his sister. "You did it. He looks amazingly happy."

"I'm so glad. It's the best thing for both restaurants, but it was a risk. The breach was long."

"Healing comes through love," the man beside her said.

"Cristiano, meet Max—my husband," Isabella said.

Cristiano looked at Isabella. "You never introduced us before."

"You weren't exactly Mr. Approachable. And then I was more concerned with getting this off the ground."

Mariella took Dante from Jackie. "I hope he didn't drool on your beautiful suit," she said.

"Not at all and it wouldn't matter if he did. Have you seen my new nephews?"

"No, but I'd like to."

They went to the stroller. The babies slept peacefully, both adorable in their little blue sweaters and hats.

"The only bad part is they'll be growing up in Australia and I won't get to see them all the time. Lizzie has promised photos every day over the Internet. When they are all older, they and Dante can play together when they visit Italy."

"A ready-made family," Mariella agreed.

"Congratulations on your own forthcoming wedding," Valentino said, coming over to Cristiano as Max and Isabella moved to talk with Scarlett and her fiancé, Lorenzo Nesta. Cristiano knew Lorenzo from his years of working at the restaurant. The change in the man since the last time he saw him was amazing. He looked younger and far happier than Cristiano had ever seen him.

"Thanks. So you're going to be a father, Val. Hard to believe," Cristiano said.

"That's something, isn't it? Never thought it would happen," he said, his gaze focused on his wife halfway across the restaurant. "You know, I almost lost her before we got things straight. Life's fleeting. Look at our mother, dying so young." His face twisted in remembered pain.

"Let it go," Cristiano said gently. "She would be happy for all of us tonight." He knew Valentino always blamed himself for not being able to save their mother, but he'd been a small child. Even adults could not have saved her. "Mariella and I are adopting Dante."

"He's not her son?" Valentino asked in surprise.

Cristiano quickly explained things, then reached out to grip his brother's shoulder. "I want to make sure my son always knows he's mine, no matter who donated the sperm. You have always been Dad's son, no matter what. And always my brother."

Valentino nodded, looking for Clara again. "I've

changed. Love and family is the most important thing to me now. And whether it's by blood or love, families evolve and are there for us."

"Even brothers we have never met before?" Cristiano asked.

"I wasn't too excited about getting to know them when I first learned they existed. But the full story is sad. Dad did his best, couldn't keep them, so sent them to live with their mother. He couldn't afford anything until after he and mamma married. They have their own problems with the situation. I hope in time all of us feel the tie I know Dad does."

"Takes some getting used to."

"No more than realizing Lisa is actually welcoming the reunification of the restaurants and that Lizzie married an Australian and had twins," Valentino said.

Cristiano laughed, feeling things were getting back to normal. "Or Isabella married."

"To a prince, no less."

"What? Neither mentioned that."

"Prince Maximilliano Di Rossi," Valentino said.

"Does Isabella plan to leave the restaurant?"

"Not a chance. She's the best thing to happen to it. Who would take over completely if not Isabella?"

"Isn't that guy with Jackie the man she dated years ago?"

"Yes. Guess love's even better the second time around. He's okay. It's the Aussie I have trouble talking with. His Italian, as far as I can tell, is limited to I love you, my darling, which he says every so often to Lizzie."

Cristiano laughed. It warmed his heart to be with his family again. The PTSD hadn't abated. He could have an episode without warning, but Mariella had been right. If he did, the family would rally round. He'd forgotten that in his first months of hiding. He wasn't perfect, but neither was anyone in the family. They all did the best they could with what they had.

Mariella was walking his way, her smile lightening his heart. He would never tire of looking at her, or being with her. Whatever the future held, they were in it together.

"So, I've met the baby twins and the older twins. Now, do you think we run the risk of twins? I have to tell you, one baby is a lot to handle."

He brushed his lips across hers. "Whatever comes, we can face it together."

"Good answer. I love you, Cristiano."

"I love you, sweetheart. What a welcome to the family, huh?"

"Well, I've met an actress, a baseball player, two ranchers, a fashion designer. How is that for a diverse family?"

"Don't forget the prince."

"What?" she exclaimed, looking around.

He explained and laughed. "I hide away from the world for a few months and everything changes."

"All for the better. A few months ago I had no one, my best friend was dead, my parents gone. Now I have you and the baby and all these amazing relatives-to-be."

"And they'll have amazing you as part of their families. I will never be able to let you know how much I love you and how much your love means to me. You've given me back my life."

"You would have reclaimed it sooner or later. I'm just glad to be a part of it now and forever. Let's just promise we won't make any of the mistakes others have made. We will be happy forever."

"Forever."

Cristiano pulled her over to one side for a kiss. Behind the pillar, his aunt was talking with a man he hadn't yet met.

"It's a new age," he heard his aunt say.

"Same old Lisa," the man retorted.

"Single, but maybe thinking of marriage. I mean, look at everyone here tonight. I never saw so much love and devotion in one room," she said.

"You always wanted to be free," he said.

"I always wanted you," she replied. "Will you marry me?"

Cristiano peered around the column. The older man with his aunt had eyes only for her. Catching his movement, they both looked at him.

"Oh, don't you breathe a word," Lisa said. She glanced at the other man. "Rafe, are you going to answer?"

"Yes, but when we are alone," he said, his eyes dancing in amusement.

"It's time for dinner," Isabella announced.

"Ah, but first one more toast," Luca said, going to stand beside his daughter.

"To the legacy of our mother, Rosa," he said, raising his glass.

"To Mamma's legacy," Lisa echoed.

"To Rosa!" the entire family said as one.

## Coming Next Month

### Available December 7, 2010

# REQUEST YOUR FREE BOOKS!
## 2 FREE NOVELS PLUS 2
# FREE GIFTS!

HARLEQUIN® *Romance*®

### From the Heart, For the Heart

**YES!** Please send me 2 FREE Harlequin® Romance novels and my 2 FREE gifts (gifts are worth about $10). After receiving them, if I don't wish to receive any more books, I can return the shipping statement marked "cancel". If I don't cancel, I will receive 6 brand-new novels every month and be billed just $3.84 per book in the U.S. or $4.24 per book in Canada. That's a savings of 15% off the cover price! It's quite a bargain! Shipping and handling is just 50¢ per book.* I understand that accepting the 2 free books and gifts places me under no obligation to buy anything. I can always return a shipment and cancel at any time. Even if I never buy another book from Harlequin, the two free books and gifts are mine to keep forever.

116/316 HDN E7T2

Name _____ (PLEASE PRINT) _____

Address _____ Apt. # _____

City _____ State/Prov. _____ Zip/Postal Code _____

Signature (if under 18, a parent or guardian must sign)

Mail to the **Harlequin Reader Service:**
**IN U.S.A.:** P.O. Box 1867, Buffalo, NY 14240-1867
**IN CANADA:** P.O. Box 609, Fort Erie, Ontario L2A 5X3

Not valid for current subscribers to Harlequin Romance books.

**Are you a subscriber to Harlequin Romance books
and want to receive the larger-print edition?
Call 1-800-873-8635 or visit www.ReaderService.com.**

* Terms and prices subject to change without notice. Prices do not include applicable taxes. Sales tax applicable in N.Y. Canadian residents will be charged applicable provincial taxes and GST. Offer not valid in Quebec. This offer is limited to one order per household. All orders subject to approval. Credit or debit balances in a customer's account(s) may be offset by any other outstanding balance owed by or to the customer. Please allow 4 to 6 weeks for delivery. Offer available while quantities last.

**Your Privacy:** Harlequin Books is committed to protecting your privacy. Our Privacy Policy is available online at www.ReaderService.com or upon request from the Reader Service. From time to time we make our lists of customers available to reputable third parties who may have a product or service of interest to you. If you would prefer we not share your name and address, please check here. ☐

**Help us get it right**—We strive for accurate, respectful and relevant communications. To clarify or modify your communication preferences, visit us at www.ReaderService.com/consumerschoice.

HR10R2

# HARLEQUIN®

## A Romance

### FOR EVERY MOOD™

Spotlight on

## Classic

Quintessential, modern love stories
that are romance at its finest.

See the next page
to enjoy a sneak peek from
the Harlequin® Romance series.

*See below for a sneak peek from our classic*
*Harlequin® Romance® line.*

**Introducing DADDY BY CHRISTMAS by Patricia Thayer.**

MIA caught sight of Jarrett when he walked into the open lobby. It was hard not to notice the man. In a charcoal business suit with a crisp white shirt and striped tie covered by a dark trench coat, he looked more Wall Street than small-town Colorado.

Mia couldn't blame him for keeping his distance. He was probably tired of taking care of her.

Besides, why would a man like Jarrett McKane be interested in her? Why would he want to take on a woman expecting a baby? Yet he'd done so many things for her. He'd been there when she'd needed him most. How could she not care about a man like that?

Heart pounding in her ears, she walked up behind him. Jarrett turned to face her. "Did you get enough sleep last night?"

"Yes, thanks to you," she said, wondering if he'd thought about their kiss. Her gaze went to his mouth, then she quickly glanced away. "And thank you for not bringing up my meltdown."

Jarrett couldn't stop looking at Mia. Blue was definitely her color, bringing out the richness of her eyes.

"What meltdown?" he said, trying hard to focus on what she was saying. "You were just exhausted from lack of sleep and worried about your baby."

He couldn't help remembering how, during the night, he'd kept going in to watch her sleep. How strange was that? "I hope you got enough rest."

She nodded. "Plenty. And you're a good neighbor for

coming to my rescue."

He tensed. Neighbor? *What neighbor kisses you like I did?* "That's me, just the full-service landlord," he said, trying to keep the sarcasm out of his voice. He started to leave, but she put her hand on his arm.

"Jarrett, what I meant was you went beyond helping me." Her eyes searched his face. "I've asked far too much of you."

"Did you hear me complain?"

She shook her head. "You should. I feel like I've taken advantage."

"Like I said, I haven't minded."

"And I'm grateful for everything…"

Grasping her hand on his arm, Jarrett leaned forward. The memory of last night's kiss had him aching for another. "I didn't do it for your gratitude, Mia."

*Gorgeous tycoon Jarrett McKane has never believed in Christmas—but he can't help being drawn to soon-to-be-mom Mia Saunders! Christmases past were spent alone…and now Jarrett may just have a fairy-tale ending for all his Christmases future!*

*Available December 2010,
only from Harlequin® Romance®.*

# SPECIAL EDITION

**USA TODAY BESTSELLING AUTHOR**

# MARIE FERRARELLA

## BRINGS YOU ANOTHER
## HEARTWARMING STORY FROM

When Lilli McCall disappeared on him
after he proposed, Kullen Manetti swore
never to fall in love again. Eight years later
Lilli is back in his life, threatening to break
down all the walls he's put up to
safeguard his heart.

# UNWRAPPING
# THE PLAYBOY

*Available December
wherever books are sold.*